Tombstone Lullaby

The wise thing for Mart Donohue to do when he sees smoke rising from a burning wagon in the heart of Apache country is to hightail it out of there as fast as he can. Instead he rides to help and finds himself accused of killing two men and the rape and murder of the fiancée of a Tombstone businessman, a girl whom he has never even seen.

The only way out of the fix is for Donohue to produce the girl alive and well. The hunt takes him through Apache Pass at a time when Geronimo is leading his rebel Chiricahua Apaches into Mexico, at the start of one of the most savage Indian campaigns America had ever seen. Then, when he does find her, the girl does not want to co-operate!

Just when he thought his troubles were over, Donohue finds they are only just beginning.

Tombstone Lullaby DA

WALT MASTERSON

A Black Horse Western

ROBERT HALE · LONDON

Typeset by
Derek Doyle & Associates, Shaw Heath
Printed and bound in Great Britain by
Antony Rowe Limited, Wiltshire

For Austin, who knows about lawmen

CHAPTER ONE

Donohue saw the smoke when he was already halfway up the Sulphur Springs Valley from the border, and the sight made him swear bitterly under his breath. The line-back mustang twitched his ears at the profanity, but he had been smelling the smoke for much longer and it made him edgy.

The valley was open north to south, and made a good road north into Arizona Territory, so it was a well trodden highway. Stagecoaches came down from the north, and benefited from the protection of Fort Bowie in Apache Pass at the area of greatest danger. Traders in their wagons used it, and mule trains used it, too.

The problem was that so did the Apache, and Apaches had a strong sense of territory. They objected to trespassers, and Apache objections ran to arrows, bullets and slow fires.

Donohue had been hoping to avoid all three by remaining inconspicuous and riding across the valley without being noticed. He knew all about Apaches and their habits because he had scouted for the cavalry at Fort Bowie, and helped bury more of the Apaches' victims than sat comfortably on a queasy stomach. Now, it looked as though his undertaking skills were going to be called on again.

The smoke came from up ahead where the trail down from the north to Tombstone and the ragged gaggle of mining settlements straddled the Dragoons and Cochise's old stronghold in the mountains straggled its way across the valley floor.

A wise man might have stayed well clear of the slowly rising column of smoke, but Donohue was not certain that there were not survivors at the foot of that smoke. It thickened even as he watched it.

He swore again, then turned the horse towards the smoke, and made a long slow curve to get to it. Once they had set something on fire, Apaches tended to go off and leave it, because they would have killed everyone there and taken what loot they valued before putting it to the torch.

Nobody, however, could predict which way they would go then, so he exercised caution.

It took him an hour to find that the smoke came from the wreckage of a burning wagon. He examined it through his binoculars from a safe distance, but there was no sign of life, so he rode up to it.

The wagon had been set on fire, but the flames had never really taken hold, and only the canopy and part of the back had burned. The wagon seat and front end were smoke stained but intact and the cargo was hardly damaged at all.

There was the corpse of a single horse still in the traces near the wagon, and the remains of straps and traces indicated there had been other horses, which had been cut free from the wagon and gone off somewhere. Without beasts to pull their wagon, the two man crew had been immobilized and, being immobile, died.

He examined the tracks around the wagon and gave a low whistle of surprise. The pursuing horses had all been shod, and no Indian war party would have been uniformly mounted on shod horses. One or two, maybe, might have stolen mounts from a ranch, but not the whole lot. There had been at least half-a-dozen pursuers.

The corpses were laid out for him to examine. Two men in their thirties, lying in the curiously boneless attitudes of the dead. Both had been shot, and their heads had then been slashed and mangled, probably in an attempt to make it look as though they had been scalped.

An Indian taking a scalp usually worked with the precision of a surgeon and took pride in it: a neat and often continuous incision separating the hair and its scalp from the rest of the head. Donohue had met one man who had actually survived the damage, and though the top of his head had been a horror, he was apparently functioning perfectly normally.

No such surgical precision had been used on these two. Their heads were terribly damaged. Each had died from a bullet wound to the body, either during the chase or the gunfight afterwards.

It had been a hard chase. The wagon had come racketing down the trail pursued by horsemen, and one of the pursuers had got close enough to shoot the lead horse. The others had been forced to stop, and the wagon had run into them. There had been a sharp exchange of gunfire – he found several cartridge cases gleaming in the dust – and then the men crouching behind the wagon had been killed.

He got close to the wagon bed and could see that it was still packed with sacks and goods. After beating at the flames with a sack he got the fire out, and examined the contents.

There were sides of bacon, sacks of flour and a couple of cases of cans of peaches and other groceries, and some sacks of beans. It looked like a supply expedition from a ranch or maybe even one of the settlements dotted among the hills, depending on shipped goods for its existence.

It was not going to get this lot. But neither was anybody else, which was strange. Indians were good looters and there was plenty to interest them here.

The bodies were dressed like normal ranch hands. Jeans, high-heeled riding boots, wool shirts and leather vests.

Sighing, he used the dead men's bandannas as receptacles, and turned out their pockets, finding pathetically little.

One had a bundle of letters, a little money and the makings of a few coffin nail cigarettes, and the other a pouch of tobacco and a pipe and similar daily requirements. Neither had much money and what they did have had not been looted.

For his own comfort, he covered their heads with charred sacking from the wagon. He might have to look at dead men, but he did not enjoy the experience.

But why had these men died?

The wagon had not been looted: Indians would have taken all the food they could find. The men's weapons had been taken, certainly, but not their tobacco. Now that the flames were out, he could by being careful, search the wagon bed itself. There was no sign of anything to make the raid worthwhile, and no sign of anything of any size having been taken from it.

There was, however, in the box beneath the wagon seat, a woman's travelling bag and two bedrolls which presumably belonged to the dead men.

He bound up the possessions in the dead men's bandannas and poked them into the bedrolls, which he tied together and rolled in a blanket. The mustang didn't much like having the extra bulk on his rump, but he put up with it.

There was no way of taking the bodies with him, so he scraped a hole under the wagon bed with a shovel with a charred handle, tumbled the corpses in, and covered them over with such stones as he could find. It was the best he could do to keep the night predators away, and they would dig down sooner or later, he knew, but perhaps by then they would have had time to send out a burial party from Tombstone.

He had heard the Earp brothers were acting as lawmen there at the moment, and they were decent enough men not to leave the corpses lying.

But it meant he had an uncomfortable journey ahead of him. He had to cut back on himself, past the Dragoon Mountains, avoiding Apaches – and Cochise's old stronghold was perched in there above the river – and report to the marshal at Tombstone. But he could do no less.

Apache eyes would have seen that smoke, and Apaches were curious folk. He was surprised they had not already shown up, but he was not betting on their absence being permanent.

On the other hand, there was the woman's travel bag. He could not simply ignore it. Somewhere back there might be a woman in hiding. Maybe she had jumped off the wagon during the early stages of the chase, and hidden herself. Maybe she had even been thrown off somehow during the hell-for-leather chase down the Sulphur Springs Valley, and had been overlooked by the pursuers.

She might even have been wounded, or even killed during the chase, in which case there would be a body there today but not after tonight, when the night-time predators had taken their toll of the corpse.

He had no choice. He had to backtrack the wagon and find where she had left it. He hoped it was not too far back. Time was against him.

And not only time. The Indians were against him, too. He found them before he had ridden more than a few miles along the backtrail, and still not come to the point where the woman – if woman there should be – had parted company with the wagon.

He found the place where the pursuers had picked up the wagon tracks, easily enough and not too far up the back trail. The raiders had come down from the rocks and gone hell-for-leather after the wagon. He could see where the driver had realized he was being followed and whipped up the horses. The longer strides of the animals and the more hectic tracks of the wheels told their own story.

The driver must have known he was being pursued right away, for the pursuers' tracks were still swinging in behind the wagon when the deeper hoof prints and the longer strides taken by the whipped up horses started.

There was still no sign of a woman's footprints leaving the wagon, no sign in fact apart from the bag that there had been a woman with the wagon at all.

He mounted the mustang again and was about to carry on his tracking when he saw, from the rocks up ahead of him, the first slowly rising puff of a smoke signal. It broke off and was repeated even while he watched. There were Indians ahead and they were smoke talking to others who might well be behind him.

He considered for a moment. Had there been a woman in the wagon? Or were the drivers merely bringing her luggage, little though it was, with them to deliver it? He was willing to take a chance if he knew there was a female, but he was not even certain there ever had been. His cursory examination of the bag had produced no clues. There was a nightdress and a change of necessary linen, a few handkerchiefs and a washing bag with soap and a flannel in it. No valuables, though there was a small bottle of lavender water which had been opened and half used.

No letters, no documents of any sort, no reticule, no valuables.

Donohue sighed, and turned the horse to the south again. He did not want to get near to the mountains, where Chiricahuas ranged, but he had to skirt south of them.

Also, in Tombstone itself there were white men who were worse than Apaches and a lot harder to pick out. Still there was nobody else present and he had it to do. He gave a resigned shrug and set the mustang on its way.

By this time, the sun was already going down, and he knew it would not be long before it would have gone. By that time, he needed a secure camp and his back against a rock. He swung the horse over towards the side of the valley and picked out a likely bunch of rocks. With Indians about, it would be a cold camp, but at least he had some of last night's camp-fire bread in his saddle-bag and some strips of jerky to make a cold supper.

The mustang, edgy and wary, would be as good a watchdog as any he could have wished for, and despite his situation, he slept relatively soundly, though the presence of the dead men's traps reminded him that to sleep too deep would be to make his rest permanent.

CHAPTER TWO

Allen Street was getting its breath back ready for the night when he rode the tired mustang up from the desert and into Tombstone. From the corner of Fremont and Sixth Street he was directed down to the courthouse where the Earps had set up a temporary office. He tied up his horse outside the sheriff's office and lockup and found a young man with a star on his shirt resting his feet on the handrail and the seat of his pants on a rocking chair.

'Need to report a couple of deaths,' he told the young man, and was rewarded with a shrug and the jerk of a thumb over his shoulder.

'Deputy's inside. Earps ain't in yet,' the youth told him laconically. He didn't actually spit tobacco juice on Donohue's boots, but he looked as though he might be considering the idea until his eyes met Donohue's flat, stony stare, and correctly saw trouble there.

Donohue stepped onto the sidewalk and the young man hurriedly took his boots of the rail and let him pass. When he told his friends about the

15

meeting later it would sound very different from the reality, but a guy had to get his self-respect back somehow.

There was a dusty hat on the deer's antler rack on the wall and a stand of rifles and shotguns behind the desk. A man in black shirt, fancy vest and black trousers was toiling over some paperwork and making heavy weather of it, and his expression when he looked up was a mixture of exasperation and relief.

'Yeah? What can I do for you?' he said.

Donohue told him about the burning wagon and the two bodies, and unloaded the blanket and its contents onto the desk. The deputy unfastened the bundles one by one, and whistled when he saw the letters.

'Cole Dadds, and if Cole was there, the other would be Henny Connolly!' he said and whistled again. 'Where d'you say you found 'em?'

Donohue walked round the desk and examined the map on the wall. It was sadly faded and the area around Tombstone was scuffed and rubbed by men trying to get their bearings. But it was clear enough in the Sulphur Springs Valley.

'Round about here,' he said, putting his finger on the little outcropping which roughly equated to the place from which he had examined the burning wagon.

'And you saw the smoke from further south?'

Donohue nodded. 'You knew them, then?' he said.

'Sure as hangment did! Two hard men, from the

16

Barratt shipping outfit. 'Hard men to kill!' He shot a glance at Donohue under his eyebrows. 'You say you come upon 'em already dead? Reckon it was Injuns done it?'

Donohue shook his head. 'Not unless they got themselves a blacksmith and forge up there in the Chiricahuas. They was all shod horses, about half a dozen or so, I reckon. They started the chase way back and that wagon driver knew he was in trouble the moment he saw them. Went off lickety-spit right away.

'Them riders only caught up with the wagon when something slowed it down. Dunno what, though.'

'And you say you buried the bodies yourself?'

'Wasn't nobody else around to do it,' Donohue told him shortly. He was tired and irritated at having the break his journey north, and there really was not much else he could tell the deputy.

Unexpectedly, the man put out his hand and shook Donohue's enthusiastically.

'Art Knowles,' he said. 'The only man around here goin' to miss 'em is Lex Barratt hisself!' he said 'Them two was trouble every time they come to town. Only worse lot are the ones who call theirselves The Cowboys. They're even givin' the Earps a hard time, and everybody round here's holdin' their breath to see what happens there.'

'I can tell you what,' Donohue told him, 'the Earps are goin' to win. I seen them work before. They're good, real good!'

He dumped the lady's bag he had found in the wagon on the desk next to the two dead men's possessions.

'Hell, there was a woman as well? You never said anything about her!' the deputy said, eyeing the bag. He reached out for it, but hesitated before opening it.

Donohue shook his head.

'No woman. I looked all round,' he said. 'Didn't even know there had been one until I found that in the wagon seat along with the bedrolls. But there were no woman's tracks, no third bedroll, no sign at all. Either she got off before the owlhoots showed up, or she learned to fly.'

'You didn't backtrack the wagon?'

'Of course! For a while! I got as far back as the place the chase started. Riders come down out of the rocks, and the wagon went off flat out straight away! Reckon they knew the riders or knew of them, and knew they was in trouble.

'But by the time I'd rode up, found the bodies, put the fire out, buried the dead, all I wanted to do was be someplace else,' Donohue assured him. 'I poked around for an hour but I couldn't find any sign of where she might have left the wagon.

'If it had been done by Chiricahuas, I might'a risked it and stayed longer, because they'd be heading away. But there was smoke talk up ahead.

'That there smoke from the wagon attracted me from miles away, and if I was curious, you can bet the Indians was, too. I never seen any, but that didn't mean they hadn't seen me. I headed for Tombstone right away.'

'But the woman?'

'I got no proof there ever was a woman. Just that

bag. No traps, no bedroll, no tracks, nothing for me to follow. Find me some hint there was a woman there, and I'll go back and look for her. Until then, I'll be at the nearest boarding-house. Where's it at?'

Knowles jerked a thumb over his shoulder and came to the door to point down the street.

'There's a place to put your horse at the OK Corral down the block a ways, and a good boarding-house there, too. Tell 'em I sent you. You can get a good meal at the Can Can, but the best food is at Nellie Cashman's just down the block at the Russ House, corner of Fifth and Toughnut. Couple of blocks that way.'

Donohue thanked him and turned the tired horse down the way the deputy had indicated. He found the OK Corral easily enough. It had an entrance on Fremont and another main gate at the other side of the block on Allen Street, the main thoroughfare of the town. A laconic old man with a broken-down hat took the horse to the back of the building and promised a bait of grain. Donohue humped his saddle across Fremont and into the boarding-house, where he argued, for the sake of appearances, over the price of a room, and left his saddle and warbag on a wooden cot.

Nellie Cashman's place was two blocks over and one along, so by the time he had got there, he had seen most of Tombstone, at least at a distance. The town was surrounded by mine workings, and the piles of tailings spilled down the hillsides.

The story of the town's name always amused him. Prospector Ed Shieffelin was a no-hope miner whose search for precious metals drew howls of derision when he announced he was goin to search in the barren lands down towards the Chiricahuas and the Dragoons. Searching for riches in lands ranged by the Apache was considered seriously bad judgement, and Ed rarely found anything worthwhile at the best of times.

'All you'll find there will be your tombstone,' warned a soldier to the sound of mocking laughter. Ed was not a man to forget or forgive the mockery, so when he made Arizona's richest silver strike he called it Tombstone and cackled over it.

He had plenty of reasons for cackling, too. The strike produced some of the richest gold and silver lodes in the Territory, and Ed settled down behind a bottle and glass to celebrate his luck. He was still celebrating.

Nellie Cashman's place at the Russ House was a single-storey, sprawling building opposite the miners' shacks from which she earned her living. She boasted that there were no cockroaches in her kitchens, and she was a good enough cook to ensure that the locals would not have minded much if there had been.

She kept her beer cold underground as well, and Donohue happily sank one schooner of it and ordered another with his steak and potatoes. He was halfway through a slice of apple pie big enough to use as a doorstop when Wyatt Earp found him.

The lawman was wearing what he called his business gear of black stovepipe trousers, black waistcoat and white shirt, with a black coat over the top. He peered at the world from between the brim of a black hat and a healthy scrubbing brush moustache. But the eyes which did the peering were steely and unwavering.

'Donohue?' he said, without bothering to introduce himself. Donohue swallowed a mouthful of pie and admitted that was his name.

The lawman pulled out a chair on the opposite side of the table, and sat down without being asked. Donohue noticed that he never turned his back on the doorway at any point, and he was sitting sideways on to the table so his gun-hand was not encumbered.

'Hear you found one of Barratt's wagons up the Sulphur Springs trail.' Earp said. 'Tell me about it.'

Donohue waved at Nellie's waitress who was carrying a big coffee pot around the tables and she refilled his cup. He pushed his chair back from the table and rolled himself a cigarette.

He described seeing the smoke, his approach to the burning wagon and his conclusions when he found it was not looted. He also mentioned the botched scalping of the two dead men, and finding the woman's bag in the wagon box.

'I tried backtracking the wagon and I found the place the killers picked it up,' he said.

'Long chase?' asked Earp. His eyes were never still, checking the door and the front windows, but he had listened intently.

'Fair to middlin',' Donohue admitted, rolling himself another cigarette. 'Gave them a good run, anyways. One of the riders got close enough to shoot the lead horse, though, and that was that. They forted up behind the wagon, but it was two agin' five

21

or six and the raiders was mobile.'

'You sure they was white men?' said Earp.

'Shod horses. Never seen Indians who all had shod horses. One or even two sometimes, but not all in a bunch. Where would they get 'em, anyways? No, I reckon they was white men and they was after that wagon come hell or high water!'

Earp looked at him hard and long. Then: 'So what happened to the woman?' he said, quietly.

Donohue put down his cigarette and took money from his pocket to pay his check.

'Didn't find no sign of her myself, just that bag on the wagon,' he said. 'There wasn't a bedroll, no clothes, nothin' else at all!

'If she was ever there, she sure done the best disappearin' act I ever did see! One thing, though: them raiders didn't get her. Not where they caught up the wagon, anyways.'

CHAPTER THREE

Earp stared at him for a moment, and Donohue felt as though he was being skinned. Then the lawman gave an unexpected grin.

'Donohue?' he said. 'Mart Donohue? Done a bit of marshalling your own self, as I hear it!'

Donohue was surprised, but not amazed. The Western territories formed a community which Easterners found hard to understand. The population was sparse and widely scattered, but wandering riders ranged it, continually on the move for one reason or another. Some were on the run from somewhere or someone, some seeking work, a home, or a woman, perhaps.

Others, like Donohue, simply had a travelling itch which would not let them rest. They paused for a while, took on work, and then moved on for reasons they were themselves unable to explain.

Time after time, Donohue had tried to put down roots, to establish a home, a place to belong to. But after a while, the old urge would not let him rest, and he found himself wondering precisely what and who were over that range of hills he could see from the stoop.

Soon after that, he was rolling his blankets again, and going to see for himself over those same mountains.

The truth was that, big though the wide open spaces of the West were, the population was small, and tended to know one another or know of one another, much better than folk in the big cities. They did not have much else to talk about at the saloon, or by the camp-fire on the range, or in the bunkhouse at the roundups. So news of men and their doings spread faster than the men themselves.

He knew about the Earps and their reputation from way back. The family was a strong band of fighting men, hard men who could cope with the lawless lands of the frontiers. There were stories about the Earps, rumours of their taking rake-offs from saloons and the other businesses of the towns they policed, but Donohue had never heard any confirmation, and if he had it would not make the Earps any different from other lawmen in the Territory.

The Earps were no worse than many of their contemporaries and often very much better. They were hard, skilful, fighting men who could control the hard, skilful fighting men who considered the new territories theirs to plunder at will.

Others might wonder who would win the impending battle between the Earps and the tough bunch who were run by the Clantons and called themselves The Cowboys. Donohue didn't. He had seen the Earps in action before, and he knew who to back in a fight.

Earp accepted a cup of coffee from Nellie Cashman when she brought it, and nodded at Donohue.

'Meet Mart Donohue, Nellie,' he said. 'Come across one of Barratt's wagons on the Sulphur Springs trail. Buried a couple of his men, too. Looks like you won't have to worry about Cole Dadds and Henny Connolly again.'

Nellie Cashman looked Donohue over as she smiled at him. She was a small, bustling figure Donohue had come across before in Tucson, where she ran Delmonico's eating-house and was a huge success. She had, for some reason, a weakness for miners and spent a good deal of her time and money on their welfare.

'Nobody else to do it,' she explained briskly, whenever she was asked, and she was right enough, there.

Mine owners liked to hire single, uncommitted men to work in the heat and danger of the mines where accidents were common and deaths frequent.

They had no intention of being saddled with widows and families to support after a mine accident – nor, equally important, a family asking awkward questions about safety.

The result was a large number of tough, hard men who needed female company and were equipped with the money to pay for it. The line of bordellos which ran down the far side of Sixth Street stood witness to their need and the women's capacity to fill it.

'Ain't much else a single woman can do, except cook and clean, and whorin' pays better,' one saloon girl had explained to Donohue over a hand of cards and a bottle of whiskey one night in one of the towns in which he had carried a gun and a badge. 'Sure, you got a few men too ready with their fists, but there's many a farmer's wife gets beat up regular, and she don't even get bought a drink for it!'

He wondered every now and again what had become of Calico Kate Prescott in the years since then, but the profession she had chosen was not a long-lived one, and she might very easily by now be dead.

Earp brought him back to the present. He was talking about the woman who seemed to have disappeared from the ambushed wagon.

'Trouble is, Barratt's been talking round town that he is bringing in his fiancée to have a big wedding here in town,' he said. 'This missing female's likely her, and Barratt's not a patient man when it comes to asking questions and getting answers.'

The lawman paused. His eyes were fixed on the window, though from Donohue's point of view there was nothing out there to see except the lights in the miners' homes across the street.

'Now, see here!' Earp said hurriedly. 'I won't have gun-fighting in the middle of town, and I don't want bullets flying here in Nellie Cashman's. Draw that gun and I'll have to. . . .'

The door banged open and Donohue understood the lawman's urgent warning. He was six feet tall himself, but the man who shouldered his way in was taller and must have weighed fifteen stone, none of it fat. He was plainly spoiling for a fight.

Black broadcloth covered shoulders which filled the door of the eating-house, and the crown of the big, flat brimmed hat brushed the lintel. There was a gold watch chain stretched across the front of the silver brocade vest, and a black bolo tie with a silver and gold medallion filled the collar of the white cotton shirt. High heeled boots added to the man's height, and under the street dust they were polished to a high gloss.

'Lex Barratt, owner of Barratt's Freight,' Earp said unnecessarily. 'It's his fiancée we were talking about.'

Barratt picked out Donohue right away and strode across the room on feet that hit the floor like pile-drivers. As he walked, he kept his right hand down at his side and his hand was concealed in the skirts of his coat. Donohue flipped the thong off the hammer of his Colt in one fluid move. Wyatt Earp could issue all the warnings he liked, but Donohue was not going to die for them.

'You're Donohue!' said Barratt, in a voice that rattled the lamp chimneys. It was not a question.

'Yeah, I know,' Donohue said, sipping his coffee with his cup cradled in both hands. At least Earp could see he was not palming his gun under the table.

'Where is Ysabella Martinez?' The voice was not as loud but it had the edge of a man who is used to getting his questions answered immediately.

Donohue, for the sake of Earp's warning, kept his voice civil, though the man's manner rubbed raw on the edge of his temper.

'I never heard of Ysabella Martinez,' he said. 'I can't help you.'

The big man glanced at Earp and obviously saw there no hint of help. He hesitated, clearly not a familiar habit with him, and plunged on.

'You're the man found my wagon and teamsters in the Sulphur Springs Valley?'

Donohue considered the question, then: 'That'd be me, yup.'

'There was a woman with them. A lady!'

Donohue considered again, nursing his coffee. Then, 'Nope. Neither woman nor lady. Two men, dead. A wagon, burning. A dead horse and a missing team. That's all I found.'

'There was more!'

Donohue detected a note of desperation in the question, and relented for a moment. Even self-important men, arrogant men, had a right to be worried about missing womenfolk.

'Sit down, Mr Barratt, and I'll tell you exactly what I found and where I found it.'

The man's hand emerged from the skirts of his coat and he placed a Greener shotgun on the table, short and ugly. Earp's shoulders visibly relaxed and he reached over, quick as a striking snake, and lifted the shotgun off the table.

Before Barratt had a chance to protest, Earp had broken the gun and shucked the cartridges onto the floor. He put the weapon back onto the table, still broken open, and Nellie Cashman, said tersely, 'I'll take that, thank you very much!' whipped it away and took it into the kitchen.

Barratt watched it go without protest, though his eyes were ugly. But he wanted information rather than trouble. Particularly trouble with the Earps.

Donohue accepted a refill for his coffee cup and waited until Barratt had also been supplied with one.

'Now, Barratt,' he said. 'This here's what I found.'

He repeated the description he had already given to the sheriff's office and to Earp, leaving nothing out and adding nothing to it.

'I found the men's blanket rolls and the woman's bag in the wagon box under the seat,' he said. 'You can still smell the smoke on them. There wasn't nothing I could do for the men except bury 'em, so I did it.

'I was worried about the woman, but there wasn't no woman's tracks round there. No sign there had ever been a woman in that wagon. Just the stores which was still there, the tracks of half a dozen shod horses, and the burning wagon. Wasn't very well alight, neither. The stores was still mostly untouched, which was another reason I don't think Indians done it.'

'But she must have been on it! She left Mexico on it, where else could she go? Maybe she jumped for it, in the chase!'

Donohue shook his head, watching the big man carefully. His distress seemed genuine enough, but this was more than just a worried groom. He had come to the restaurant with a hidden shotgun, and in the confines of the room it would have been lethal. Donohue was pretty sure the only reason Barratt hadn't used it was that Earp was unexpectedly present when he arrived.

But there were men and their wives present in the room. The shotgun would have been bound to cut down some of the bystanders if the big man had fired it.

'I am sorry for your loss,' he said, 'but she simply was not there. I backtracked the wagon as far as I could – back beyond the place where the owlhoots started chasin' it – and there wasn't no signs of your fiancée. No tracks, no sign that she had jumped from the wagon, no other clues a-tall!'

It wasn't enough for the big man.

'But what do you think? Where could she have gone?' The edge was back in his voice, now. The worry had left his eyes and they were taking on a more calculating look.

'I ain't got no idea, Barratt. She wasn't on it, and I couldn't find no place she had left it. Not in the time I had. There was smoke talk in the hills north of there, and a smudge down south. After an hour or so, I lit out.

'The rest you know.'

The big man gazed at him for a moment, then his stare dropped. He shrugged.

'That will have to do, I suppose. Marshal.'

Earp nodded curtly. 'Barratt,' he acknowledged. There was no warmth in the tone, and Donohue wondered what was between the two men.

Barratt picked up his shotgun from the kitchen and walked out of the front door without looking back. As the door closed, Donohue heard the click of the breech shutting and knew the weapon was now reloaded. Earp's eyes never left Barratt while he was within sight and he spoke without looking at Donohue.

'Don't think this is over, Donohue! He didn't bring that shotgun as a gesture. He's got double-ought ball in there, and he is not afraid to use it. Watch your back while you are in Tombstone, and everywhere else when you are not.'

Donohue had the same impression. He had seen eyes like that once on a mountain lion, and there was neither pity nor remorse in them.

It suddenly occurred to him that the doomed driver and his mate on that wagon had known their pursuers, might have guessed what the future held for them, had been running for their lives.

It was a thought, and it kept him out of the shadows on his way back to the boarding-house. In this savage outpost of civilization, he felt more in danger than out on the open ground where Indians and the animals were at least easily identified dangers.

CHAPTER FOUR

The bottom end of Fremont Street was in darkness, away from the lanterns which made an attempt at illuminating the main streets, but there was light enough from the windows looking onto it for him to find the alley which led down to the boarding-house. He flicked a match on his thumb nail to see his way down the alley, then dropped it underfoot as soon as he was sure the narrow passage was empty.

The boarding-house door was lit through glass panels from inside, and he reached for the door handle and stumbled over something lying on the step.

Unwilling to light himself up again, he bent and peered in the reflected light from the door and found he had stumbled over his own saddle and warbag. It had been stacked neatly on the porch.

Surprised, he knocked on the door, though without result.

'Hello, the house!' he called. There was no response, but the light within went out.

'Say something, if it's only goodbye!' he said, and

looked over his shoulder at the suddenly darkened alleyway. He already felt uneasy and for some reason the sound of music and raucous laughter from the saloons only a street away emphasized the isolation of his position here.

Fremont was what passed in Tombstone for the business quarter, many of the buildings were offices, open during the day, but dark and closed up now. If he had planned an ambush he could not have chosen a better setting himself.

Away from the noise of the main streets a shot would hardly be noticed except by the local inhabitants and they would have more sense than to investigate before morning. Random shots could kill a well-meaning local as easily as a prowling assassin.

He picked up his warbag and threw it over his shoulder, and hefted the saddle with his left hand. Then he took the Winchester in his right and swung it like a sabre. Finally, he walked down the alleyway to Fremont Street.

Nobody stood in his way, and his tensely attuned hearing detected no footsteps behind him in the dark. Yet there was danger here. His instinct for self preservation was certain of it, and by listening to that instinct, Donohue had lived through three wars and a lifetime of trouble.

He emerged into Fremont Street and turned towards the sheriff's office, a pool of light in the darkness. Nobody stood in his way, and a glance over his shoulder showed him no sinister silhouettes against the few lighted windows.

Yet his back itched between the shoulder blades,

and he trusted that itch.

He was just outside the deeply recessed doorway of one of the offices along the block and by a sudden instinct, dropped his saddle into it, and sat down on the saddle. It left him both concealed from anybody following him and lower than they would expect him to be.

The shots came immediately, two flat reports from a handgun, and simultaneously he heard the slugs slap into the adobe wall, one above his head and the other out on the street wall. The din from Allen Street did not even pause. A woman laughed drunkenly, and a man shouted. There was another shot, a couple of blocks away and a man cried out hoarsely.

For a second, he sat quietly, then at the edge of hearing, caught a whisper of movement out on the sidewalk. There was a faint scuff of sound as somebody's coat brushed on the adobe at the doorway, and he swung the rifle viciously at knee height and had the satisfaction of feeling the barrel bite into bone.

There was an agonized yell, and he straightened up and struck sideways again, this time catching the man on the arm.

There was a guttural grunt of pain which told him where the head was, and his third slash hit something that sounded like wood, but he knew was bone. There was a clatter, and the shadowy figure staggered out into the street, moving at a shambling run, but before he could extricate himself from his saddle and traps it was gone into the shadows at the other side of the street near the alleyway to the OK Corral.

He waited, still in the shadow of the doorway until somebody carrying a lantern emerged from the sheriff's office and peered down the street. He could see the outline of a shotgun muzzle, and called immediately, 'Hello! Hello, the light!'

The shotgun swing towards him and Art Knowles's voice replied, 'Who's there? Speak up!'

'It's Donohue! Hold your fire, I'm comin' in!'

'You alone?' called the deputy.

'Far as I know.'

'Come ahead, then!' But the muzzle of the shotgun followed him into the aura of light cast by the lantern.

Knowles looked at the saddle and warbag with interest.

'Thought I told you where to get a room. Ma Beckles full, or somethin'? She ain't usually that busy, this time o' year.'

Donohue shifted his belongings into the office and dumped the saddle on the floor in a corner, laid his Winchester and his warbag on the desk.

'You,' he said, 'got a right lively town here! Right lively!'

'That we do, mister,' grinned the deputy. 'Earp find you? We told him Nellie Cashman's was the likeliest place. Seemed to me you might even know her.'

'Used to eat at Delmonico's in Tucson when she was there,' acknowledged Donohue. 'Can't claim to know her well, just enough to respect her mightily. A whole lot of woman, is Nellie.'

The deputy leaned forward and tipped Donohue's hat back so he could see his face in the light of the lantern. He whistled softly.

'You been irritatin' the wrong people, fella,' he said. 'Wait there and I'll get you some water. I been heatin' some up for coffee.'

He poured some water from the kettle on the stove into a tin basin and tore a strip of rag from the end of an old sheet hanging from a nail. As a first aid station, it left a lot to be desired, but it was adequate to mop Donohue's face.

The deputy brought him the shaving mirror from the wash stand in the corner, and held it while Donohue examined his face. It was dotted down the side with little drops of blood, and when he wiped it down with the wet rag, it stung mightily. There was a residue of little flecks of gravel on the towel in the blood, and he realized it must be powdered adobe thrown out by the last shot at him.

'Even the walls shoot back, here, friend,' he told the deputy, wincing. The man handed him a flat flask of whiskey and he soaked some into the cloth and used it as disinfectant for the tiny wounds on his face. It stung like fire, and he sucked in a few sharp breaths. The deputy chuckled.

'I've seen men with arms cut off make less fuss. But whiskey in gravel spatter sure do make a man jump around like a bug on a hot plate. Lucky you didn't get it in the eye!' He took the used water away and threw it out of the back door, then closed the door and barred it.

'Now you're mended, what happened?' he said.

Donohue gave him a terse account of the events of the last couple of hours. The deputy whistled.

'Well, I heard somebody put the word out on you a couple of hours back while I was doin' my rounds,' he said. 'Been lookin' for you off and on ever since. You sure have upset somebody in town. And only been here less than half a day!'

Donohue pressed him, but Knowles clearly did not know any more than he had said, which was that there was said to be $500 on Donohue's head for the kidnap of the missing woman. He did not know who had posted the reward and he did not know why, but he was careful to press home the warning.

'Five hundred would buy you a private army, horse, foot and guns complete, in this town, friend,' he said. 'Whoever posted you wants you bad, and from what you say, it's already started. Best you stay here tonight. I got nobody in the cells yet, and the beds in there are clean enough. Wyatt sometimes sleeps here hisself, and he's a mite particular where he lays his head.'

He led the way through the heavy wooden door at the back of the office, into a short corridor off which three cells opened. Two contained four bunks each. Knowles pulled open the doorway to the first cell. It was partitioned from the other two with a wooden plank wall screwed to the bars to give privacy, and the only one with a keyhole on the inside of the grille door as well as the outside.

Donohue threw his saddle in the corner, and his bag on the bed, and followed the deputy back into the outer office. Knowles made coffee and passed a tin of sugar across.

'You done walked into a real swarm of trouble in

37

this town, friend,' he said, putting his feet on the desk and sipping his coffee carefully. Drinking hot coffee from a tin cup was an art if a man wanted to avoid burning his lips, and Knowles clearly had plenty of practice.

Over the next hours, Knowles rambled happily on about the situation in Tombstone, a conversation which sounded more like a combat report than news of a small town.

'Tombstone only bin here for a couple o' years,' he said. 'Up to now, we got two dance halls, twelve gambling-houses, twenty saloons, more drink dens than you could shake a stick at, and enough bordellos to make an A-rab sheikh happy!'

He chortled and sipped his coffee again.

'Hell, we even got a real live belly dancer down at the Bird Cage. Big girl, and when she shakes her bozzoom, a man could go blind tryin' to keep his eyes on it!'

'What's goin' on between the Earps and the town? I hear there's trouble and Wyatt seemed right jumpy when he was talkin' to Barratt.'

'Barratt? You seen him already? For my money, he's the one put the word out on you. You was lucky he wasn't totin' his shotgun. He's hell on wheels with that Greener.'

Donohue explained the meeting at Nellie Cashman's and the deputy nodded with understanding.

'You was lucky Wyatt was there, friend. When Barratt goes on the prod, he means it.'

Donohue brought him back to the town's situation

and the reason for the antagonism between the Earps and the rest.

'It ain't everybody again' 'em. It's the bunch they call The Cowboys makes the trouble. They was here long before the town, and they reckon this is their territory. They sell their beef to Tombstone, now, as well as the army, and they kinda reckon the town's theirs to do what they want.'

'Who are they?'

'Clantons and the McLaurys mainly. Old man Ike Clanton, and his sons Phineas and Billy's the main ones, and the McLaury boys, Frank and Tom. They got outfits and ranch out of town.

'Bin their territory up until Ed Schieffelin struck silver here, and then Tombstone jes' growed! Ike and his crew simply can't accept that things is changin'. Folks in town want to be able to walk down the street without some drunk cowboy blastin' off just to hear the bullets bang.'

Right on cue, a barrage of shots sounded out on the street, and Knowles swore and grabbed for his hat.

'See what I mean? Some nights it's like Gettysburg in here. You better wait until I get back!'

He reached for the door, then paused.

'Wyatt said you'd carried a badge in a coupla towns before now. You don't feel like backin' me up on this one, do you?'

Donohue reached for his hat, and grinned.

'Do I get paid for it?'

'Yup! Usual rates – here, catch.' He tossed a badge from the desk drawer.

'Do you solemnly swear—?'

'Yeah!' said Donohue. 'Douse the light before you open that door.'

They stepped out into the night, alive with shouts, screams and shots. Tombstone was off on its nightly Armageddon.

CHAPTER FIVE

It was a cold night, and he was glad of the leather coat buttoned up to his chin. He carried one of the office double-barrelled Greeners loaded with double-ought cartridge which the deputy guaranteed would stop one bear or two Tombstone troublemakers, without bothering to find out that Donohue had been shooting them since he was knee-high.

It was after midnight, now, and though the major saloons were still roaring like lions, most of the smaller places were running down. The red light district on the other hand was bouncing with life. He heard laughter both bass and falsetto, and carefully stayed away from the front of the cat-houses.

He would not have any woman mistreated, no matter what her way of life, but he was also aware that when the blood was hot, and tempers fast, the sight of a law officer could spark the very trouble he was trying to avoid.

There were a couple of dead drunks along the line of shacks the miners used, and he checked they were breathing and left them alone, too.

Shouting and threats from one of the Mexican cantinas made him poke his head round the door, but withdraw it quickly when he discovered that one of the voices was from a husky voiced Mexican woman with muscles like a prize fighter and a tousled mass of black hair. She was winning the fight, which was hardly surprising, since she was wielding a cast-iron skillet three feet across, and her adversary had only his hands to defend himself.

He saw a couple of miners home to their shacks, though neither of them would remember it in the morning, peered down several alleyways and decided not to investigate further, and exchanged a reassuring wave with Knowles as the man emerged into enough light to recognize him.

At the foot of another cross street, he found himself facing a man with a long black coat and a heavy moustache, wearing a star. Knowles emerged from the shadows opposite to greet them both.

'Donohue, this is Virgil Earp, Wyatt's brother and the city marshal,' he said. 'Virgil, this is Donohue. Wyatt met him earlier. He's been thrown out of his lodgings, and there's a price—'

'On his head. I know!' said Virgil Earp. 'What's he doin' wearin' a badge?'

Knowles looked embarrassed in the uncertain light from a lantern outside the nearest saloon.

'Had to keep him with me, and swearin' him in as a deputy means he earns his keep,' said Knowles. 'Besides, I already seen one man shot in mistake for him.'

Earp looked at them both, shrugged and made to move on.

'Business of the sheriff's office, then, not the marshal,' he said. 'But he stays with you and you can explain it to Behan. I got enough problems with him a'ready.'

Behan, explained Knowles, as they retraced their steps cautiously towards the jail, was the sheriff of Tombstone, who had thrown in his lot with The Cowboys and Clanton/McLaury faction.

'Don't get involved,' he advised. 'Both sides think they're right, but when it comes right down to it, I ain't sure either of 'em is. Seems to me Tombstone miners moved in on cattle land, but, at the same time, the ranchers can't just wander around like Johnny Gamecock the way they used to.'

Donohue nodded noncommittally. So far as he could make out, Tombstone was headed for a fair-to-middling civil war, and the winners would write the history. He did not want to be consumed by either side.

Knowles let him back into the office to find Wyatt Earp already there, and coffee on the stove.

'I know of at least one man killed in mistake for you already,' the lawman told him. 'You're bad news to Tombstone and we got enough of our own,' he said to Donohue curtly. 'I haven't got time or the jurisdiction, if it comes to that, to investigate what happened out in the Sulphur Springs Valley.'

Donohue nodded. He unpinned the star from his clothes and threw it back on the desk.

'I'll ride out in the morning,' he said. 'I still can't

figure out what happened to the girl, or even if she was ever on that wagon. If I go back there and try again, maybe I'll come across her. If so, I'll bring her back here, and you can sort out the mess.'

He was tired through to the bone, bitterly angry that he had allowed himself to be involved in an affair which was none of his business, and frustrated that, being involved, he needed to account for himself.

'So if you find her, you'll bring her back. What if you don't find her?' asked Earp.

'Then I won't!' said Donohue shortly, and shouldered his way through to his bed in the end cell.

It was still dark when he awakened, and the air was chill even in the cell. He rolled out of his blankets, pulled on his clothes and without bothering to wash, packed his saddle and bag and went out into the office.

Knowles had gone, presumably to his own bed, and there was a man he had never seen before sitting at the desk laboriously filling in a form with the stub of a pencil. He looked up at Donohue and nodded, pointing his pencil at the stove.

'Coffee in the pot,' he said. 'You can get breakfast at Chong's down near the Birdcage, but Art says don't sit with your back to the door. They know you ain't dead. Your horse has been moved from the OK to Smith's on the opposite side of Allen Street. Knowles says good luck, and watch your back.'

Donohue thanked him and fortified himself with coffee before he humped his saddle and traps across the street and over to the corral. He did not risk staying long enough to have breakfast, but threw his saddle over the mustang and his leg over the saddle.

It was a cold morning, and he pulled his neck down into his collar as he turned the horse's head away from the closed, cold saloons and towards the Sulphur Springs Valley once again.

From the edge of town, interested eyes watched him go, and a lad was sent to hammer on Lex Barratt's door. For once, he was rewarded with a silver dollar instead of a clout on the ear. Barratt was interested in Donohue's movements, and he was willing to pay good money for information on them.

CHAPTER SIX

There was a cloud of dust in the main street of Turquoise as Donohue rode in, and a dust devil whirling down a side street. The whole town seemed to have been made of dust, though it thrived on it.

A sign on the front of a square, wooden building halfway down the street sandwiched between a general store and a saloon said, simply: FOOD in white painted letters across one of the two windows and: GOOD FOOD on the other. Both turned out to be true, and he sat at the long trestle table down the centre of the room, his back to the wall with a good view of his horse, hitched at the rail out front near a water trough, and both the front door and the counter between the eating room and the kitchen.

A large cheerful black man called Rodney roared a greeting as he came in, and managed to take his order and hand him a coffee cup without taking his attention from the array of frying pans on a big, iron range along the back wall.

He ordered ham and eggs with fried potatoes and pancakes on the side, and filled his cup from a large coffee urn over a spirit lamp. There was molasses to sweeten it and after burning his mouth on the scalding coffee he added cream as well.

Rodney noted his choice of seat with a knowing eye, and unfussily moved a sawn off shotgun from under the counter to a nail on the wall by the range.

Donohue sipped his coffee, and refilled it and his meal arrived with such speed he suspected Rodney had transferred somebody else's order to him. Men with careful eyes who chose seats with their back to the wall and a good view of the street were not unfamiliar in Turquoise, and were usually accompanied by gunfire, and Rodney wanted this customer fed and out as fast as possible.

Rodney was gratified at the speed at which his food disappeared, and accepted the thrown fifty-cent piece by way of a tip with a gracious inclination of the head. Rodney was a legend in his own lifetime, and he intended that lifetime should continue as long as possible.

Donohue had not seen anything in the street which indicated trouble, but he was a careful man, so with a murmured apology to Rodney, he put his hand on the counter, vaulted over and left the restaurant through the rear door, crossed the little fenced yard at the rear, and hopped over the fence at the opposite end from the gate.

Nothing happened.

He eased down the alleyway behind the buildings which fronted onto the street, and came back to the main street between two buildings further down. His careful survey of the street revealed only dust devils and a couple of horses standing hipshot and heads down at the hitching rail outside the sheriff's office opposite. They had not been visible from his seat in the restaurant.

The horses had not been there when Donohue arrived in town, however, and he eased back down the alley, went back up the block until he came to an empty site with some half-built adobe walls round it, and looked out.

There was a window in the upper storey of the saloon opposite which was several inches open, and which he remembered as being closed when he rode in. The whirling dust and the cold wind made it highly unlikely anybody would open it for fresh air, so he assumed whoever pursued him had caught up.

He had stopped in Turquoise as much to find out if he was being followed as for any other reason, so he was not particularly surprised. He found it easier to deal with an identified threat out in the open than one buried in a crowd in a main thoroughfare like Allen Street.

What he now needed to know was the where-abouts of the rider of the second horse. If they had split up – and why send two men if they stuck together in the same place? – where was number two?

He drew back from the corner while he consid-ered it, and used the time to roll himself a cigarette and twist the end. He was just leaning forward to light the smoke, when it occurred to him where the second man might – must – be.

He was just in time to turn the slight inclination of

his head into a full forward roll, dropping the cigarette and losing his hat while he clawed for his gun. Dust erupted from the adobe wall behind him as he did so and the flat report of a rifle coincided with the spiteful whine of a ricochet.

Donohue did not have time to work out precisely where the sniper was. He rolled and rolled again until he was hard up against the low far wall of the enclosure, the long barrelled Colt coming easily into his hand.

He eased himself up slightly until he could see over the wall at the front, in time to see a rifle barrel extend slowly from between the sill and the window frame. It was not a long shot and he could see shadow within the room of the man at the other end of the rifle.

His hat was lying just out of arm's reach, and he extended his leg and hooked it closer without taking his eyes off the rifle barrel. There was a lump of unfinished adobe just to his front, and he tucked up behind it, drew the knife from his boot and reached out with his left hand to hold the hat up with it.

Instantly the rifle banged out and as instantly he fired at the half seen presence in the window. The glass pane shattered, a man cried out hoarsely and the rifle fell out over the sill and rattled on the sidewalk.

Donohue heard a door slam, and running feet on the boards on his side of the street, and peered cautiously out from behind his friendly adobe buttress. He was just in time to see one of the horses in front of the sheriff's office rear away from the hitching rail, blocking his view as a man threw himself into the saddle of the other animal, and took off down the street like a race-winner.

He jumped to his feet, but the loose horse blocked his aim, and his own animal, startled by the commotion, began to plunge and tug at his rein.

Down the street another door slammed and there was shouting as he came out cautiously on to the sidewalk. A man ran towards him, saw the gun in his hand, then skidded to a stop, holding his hands wide, to show he had no weapon in his grip.

He was wearing a star on his vest, and was half shaven, one side of his face shiny with the new-scraped skin and the other, ludicrously, wearing a Father Christmas beard of shaving soap.

'Hold your fire!' he shouted. 'I'm Sheriff Kemp! I'm the law!'

Donohue straightened up, opened the Colt's loading gate and replaced the spent cartridge. Then he spun the cylinder to make sure it was running free, and dropped the weapon back into its holster.

'If you are the law,' he said, in a voice dripping with exasperation, 'where the hell was you when they were shootin' at me?'

The lawman looked down at himself, and scrubbed the shaving soap off his face with one hand. He was carrying his gunbelt looped over his shoulder, pistol still in the holster, and he swung the belt around his hips and fastened the big, brass buckle. Settling his weapon into place, he started to draw it, and stopped when Donohue put his hand back onto the butt of his Colt.

'Hell, mister,' he said. 'Didn't you hear me? I'm the law!'

'I just rode up from Tombstone, and they got all the law I can handle at the moment right there! There's Cowboy law, sheriff's law and Earp law and even the law of averages there! What law do you reckon you are?'

The lawman was a grizzled, tanned man with a grey stubble where the barber had been interrupted. He had regained his dignity, and was not about to have it shaken again. He reached out and pointed with his left hand without taking his right away from his gun.

'Take your gun out and put it on the ground!' he said.

'No, siree! My gun stays where it is! I ain't got no beef with you, Sheriff. Let's leave it that way!'

He pointed at the rifle lying on the sidewalk.

'Guy in the upstairs room there took one shot at me, and his partner who just left town like his tail was a-fire took another. One's all any man gets! After that, I start shootin' back!'

'How many shots missin' from that sidearm o' yourn?' asked the sheriff. He was still using his left hand to point.

'I didn't shoot but once, but you just saw me reload it, so there's no point in checking the loads. There's six in there, and all you could tell is that she's been fired, which I don't deny.'

The tension was eased when another man with a badge came out of the saloon next to the sheriff's office.

'Dead,' he said without being questioned. 'Went through his right eye and took the back of his head clean out. That was shootin', mister!'

He bent down and picked up the rifle from the ground. It was still cocked, and he opened the action and took out the live shell from the breech. Then he worked the action spilling the cartridges into the dust. There were ten of them. He picked them up and slipped them into his pocket.

'Winchester saddle carbine. Thirteen in the magazine so he fired twice,' he said. 'I heard three rifle shots afore I heard your handgun, mister.'

Donohue nodded. 'There was another shooter. He darn' near nailed me, too! I got careless figuring out where this guy was.' He gestured at the upstairs window.

The sheriff gestured and pointed at the saloon door.

'We'll go and have a look,' he said. 'Maybe you'll know him, if there's enough left of his head.'

Donohue noticed he gestured with his right hand, and took it to mean that he was being trusted. He thought wryly that only twenty four hours ago, before he did the right 'good citizen' thing, he had taken it for granted that he would be trusted anywhere.

But he relaxed enough to accompany the sheriff and his deputy through the saloon and up the stairs under the sardonic stare of the early morning barman and the saloon swamper. The swamper sighed wearily and brought his bucket and mop up the stairs behind them.

The dead man had been turned on his back by the

deputy and his face was much less damaged than the back of his head, though one eye was a red hole. Donohue had never seen him before to the best of his knowledge, and he said so.

Kemp took him back to his office, to explain his story more fully.

'Funny kind of a tale, that,' admitted the lawman, scratching at the unshaven half of his jaw. 'How come they was so all-fired keen on seein' you dead? And if they want to see you dead, how come you ain't? If Tombstone's had time to develop a natural talent, it's killin'.'

'I've had time to develop a talent for stayin' alive, that's how come,' Donohue told him easily. 'Leads to a long life and happiness. Pure luck, I guess.'

'And a good eye for the fall o' shot,' agreed the lawman. 'What you goin' to do now?'

'Well, now that I've had a chance to tell the truth of it to the law, I'm goin' back to that there burned-out wagon and backtrack it to find out what happened to the girl they say was in it. She sure weren't there when I found it and she left no tracks. I reckon she must have got off back up the line a bit, and if I can get there before it rains, I'll have some chance of finding the tracks. Find the tracks and I can find the girl. It's the only thing that will get me off the hook in Tombstone.'

'And if she turned out to be dead anyhow?'

'Then I ain't comin' back,' Donohue told him. 'I got no good news and when they hear bad, folks down Tombstone way get right unfriendly.'

CHAPTER SEVEN

There was dust in the air as he turned the mustang's head north along the trail which led up Sulphur Springs Valley, and he had no idea whether it was the fitful wind, the remains of the trail of one of his shadows, or, worst of all, Apaches.

He was acutely conscious of the nearness of Cochise's own stronghold to his north and he could look up into the mountains which concealed it. He had little doubt that the Apaches knew he was around, and he would give anything to be somewhere else, but he was growing more and more convinced that the girl existed, that she was alive and that she was somewhere up ahead of him.

He angled down out of the foothills and let the mustang pick his own easier trail on the valley floor. After a while he came across his own tracks in the trail heading for Tombstone, and looked carefully at them for a while when he noticed that the tracks of several unshod ponies paralleled them for a while.

The Indians had apparently come across his sign when they came in their turn to investigate the column of smoke from the burning wagon. They had looted what they could from the wagon for it was stripped bare, though the graves of the two white men remained untouched, save by animals. There had been some scraping at the earth under the wagon bed but the bodies had not been reached. He left them well alone.

The Indians had come in from the north, which meant that they had followed him down the valley from the ambush site. They had looted the wagon, then carried on following his tracks, but either not caught up with him or seen him, and were not bothered. That was unlike Apaches unless they had found something more important or more fun to do.

A woman, for instance.

Donohue's mind shied away from why a woman might be more interesting and more fun to the Apache mind, but there was nothing to indicate that the warriors might have had the missing woman with them, so he looked carefully around, mounted the horse, and carried on following his own tracks to the north.

Apart from keeping a casual eye on his tracks he did not pay them special attention until he arrived at the point where the riders had come down from the rocks to chase the wagon.

This time, he backtracked the riders and found a place where they had waited for the wagon. There were tracks and droppings from their horses, a place where they had built a fire, and a pile of coffee grounds where they had emptied their pot. There were a couple of ends of chewed over jerky, and a discarded piece of camp-fire bread, so they had spent more than a couple of hours here, or they would not have bothered to have a meal.

It was hardly likely, therefore, that the men had been following the wagon. They had been waiting for it, and the wagon team either did not know them, or did know them and feared them. Rightly, from the end result.

He found a small patch of cigarette ends and a cigar stub, which indicated that the men were not experienced in Indian country, for Donohue knew Comanche trackers who could follow a man for a mile simply by working their way down the drift of his cigar smoke. It hung in the air on a still day for up to an hour.

There was nothing else on the camp site for him, so, carefully paralleling their tracks, he backtracked the pursuers' route to the ambush site. It swung back towards the Dragoons and uncomfortably close to Cochise's old stronghold.

Since they had not had the girl with them when they ambushed the wagon, there didn't seem to be any reason to backtrack further, particularly in such a perilous location. Natchez and his Apache band were supposed to be around, he had learned from the breakfast customers at Rodney's, and had been reported raiding even close up to Fort Bowie, with its regular heavy patrols.

'But if he's at Apache Pass he ain't down in Sulphur Springs Valley,' he told himself reassuringly, and wished he could not feel eyes boring into his back. Natchez might have been in Apache Pass two or three days ago, but an Apache in a hurry could cover nearly fifty miles on foot in twenty-four hours, and Apache Pass was nothing like fifty miles away.

The tracks of the wagon ran back up the trail and occasionally to one side of it when the ground had been badly rutted, with the horses pulling well at a regular pace. It did not look as though the men had been in any particular hurry, which was odd in itself if they had been bringing Señorita Ysabella Martinez to her waiting groom.

He carried on following the tracks until he had topped out from the valley and the wagon tracks swung away towards Fort Bowie in the throat of Apache Pass.

He had friends at Bowie who might be able to hand on more news, so he sent the mustang along the trail at an easy distance-eating lope, with half an eye on the wagon track and the rest of his attention on the surroundings.

What puzzled him was the direction taken by the wagon. If it had come up from Mexico, why on earth was he tracking it in the opposite direction? He was certain he had got the right wagon, because one of the tyres was cracked, and the crack left a signature as easy to recognize as a smoke signal.

It was almost as though the girl was being brought on a roundabout route deliberately to slow her down. Or for some other reason.

But what? He considered the matter over his cold camp meal of jerky and water that night, and could not work it out. But his sense of unease grew.

*

There were the remains of a wickiup in the pass near the Butterfield stage station where an inexperienced Lieutenant George Bascom had managed to turn Cochise from a reluctantly tolerant Indian into a furiously angry and deadly enemy by kidnapping his relatives.

Bascom had survived the incident, but not the Civil War. The Indian trouble he had started led to the deaths of many, and the bitterness the incident left behind it was still taking its toll twenty years later. Donohue spat at a scurrying scorpion in disgust, and missed it to his further disgust.

He rode with caution up to the spring below the fort, and watered his horse and refilled his canteen at the spring. There were fresh moccasin prints in the mud by the running rill, and a stone was overturned on the little pathway up the other side.

He drew his Colt and rode with it in his hand resting on his thigh as he went up the narrow track to the fort above, and saw a patrol just setting out towards him as he did so. There was little room on the trail, so he pulled aside into a bay in the trees to let it pass him, and was not surprised when the lieutenant leading called out his name.

'You coming back to the colours, Irish?' Lieutenant Petersen asked him with interest. Donohue had scouted for Petersen many times and liked and respected the Swede. He was a good woodsman as well as a good soldier and seldom lost a man in a country notorious for its death-rate.

'Not this time, Lieutenant,' Donohue told him. 'This time I'm lookin' for a woman gone missin' up this way. Lady name o' Ysabelle Martinez, You seen her?'

'Seen her? I fell in love, horse, foot and baggage!' the lieutenant told him with a broad grin. 'If it wasn't for the army I'd have carried her off to my castle in the mountains and made an honest woman of her!'

It was the first Donohue had heard a first hand impression of the woman Barratt had apparently chosen as a wife.

'Tell me about her,' he said, and the lieutenant looked uneasily back at the patrol filing past them.

'Be glad to, Irish, but I got to get this lot to get down to Fort Huachuca. They're needed for some kind of combined operation. Tell you what, call in at the post commissary. There's a barman there talked to her a whole heap. His name's Wilcox, Des Wilcox. He'll put you right. Tell him I sent you!'

He turned and started to follow his command down the pass past the spring, then looked back suddenly.

'Why don't you sign up again, Irish? There's plenty of action coming! New leader called Goyathlay's rousing up the San Carlos reservation Apaches, and the Chiricahuas are just as troublesome. There's plenty of 'em round here, too!'

'There's been some at the spring!' Donohue told him. 'Unless you know about them already, keep your heads down and your eyes peeled. They weren't botherin' to hide their tracks, so they must feel pretty confident. And confident Apaches where they didn't ought to be spells trouble!'

He stopped as a second thought struck him.

'Also, Goyathlay's not a new leader! That's Geronimo's Indian name!'

The soldier waved his hand to show he had heard, and vanished down the pass in pursuit of his command. Donohue listened for a few minutes, but heard no shooting and assumed either the Apaches had thought the better of it this close to the fort or had gone about whatever other business they had.

It did not sound good, but he had a girl to find and he needed to do it right quickly. He rode on up the pass to where he could see the outline of the arsenal and the trading post of Fort Bowie outlined in the notch on the skyline.

CHAPTER EIGHT

The sentry on the arsenal roof watched him come up the winding road from the spring, and when he was within easy range, challenged him. Donohue knew him by name and said, 'Good man, Somerset! Glad to see you doin' your duty by the United States Army! Keep it up!'

The sentry, grinning broadly, rested his carbine on his hip while he invited the former scout, in terms biological and anatomically unlikely, to look after himself.

'Y'all come back to sign up for a real man's life?' he enquired. 'General could do with a real scout these days. Ol' Buffalo Harris cashed his chips last month drinkin' bad water. We found him tied to his saddle tryin' to get back to the post, but he only lived long enough to tell us not to rely on Mesquite Tank, then he showed us why not, and died doin' it. Nasty way to go.'

'Geronimo knows a nastier, and I hear he's jumped the reservation,' Donohue retorted, and the sentry grinned.

'That he has. Nobody knows which way he jumped, though. Lieutenant Petersen went off earlier to do a sweep down towards Huachuca just now. You musta passed him on the trail.'

There was a bellow of rage from somewhere behind the sentry and he turned suddenly into a pillar of stone while a voice which said very loudly, 'Sergeant!' ran through his ancestry, pretensions, chances of promotion and hope of resurrection.

A grizzled man whose face seemed to have been hacked out of granite, came round the corner of the building, still bellowing, and broke off instantly as he recognized Donohue.

'Marty Donohue, me lad!' Sergeant Heffernan who had been born in Brooklyn and was about as Irish as Cochise, had spent his career in the army perfecting an Irish brogue which would have embarrassed a music hall comedian. It was noticeable that he dropped it when in Donohue's company, and the scout suspected it was because Heffernan was afraid he would one day expose him as a fake Irishman.

Fake Irishman he might have been, but he was a very real and professional soldier, and Donohue respected and liked him.

'Are you comin' back to the colours, laddie? The colonel will be delighted to see ye if you are.'

Donohue dismounted to shake hands and allowed himself to be led through the fort gates and onto the huge parade ground. In the far corner was a detachment of men drilling smartly in the winter sun, a strict exercise which for once was not being resented. It kept the men warm.

'Promising bunch of lads, just out from the East,' Heffernan told him as he led the way around the parade ground. 'They'll make soldiers if Geronimo will just let me have the time to work me subtle magic on the sons o' Satan.'

He waited while Donohue tied his horse to the hitching rail by the foot of the steps of the store and saloon, and led the way up the steps. For once, he, a stout and devoted drinker, did not drink.

'Not on duty, and until that red bastard is back where he should be, we're all on duty up here. I'll buy you a cold beer, though. Good beer up here!'

He was right, and Donohue gratefully sank a half of it before he put the glass down.

'I have to report to the commanding officer, Heff,' he said. 'There are fresh pony tracks down round the spring, and they are of unshod mounts.'

The sergeant nodded gravely, waited for him to finish his beer, then led the way to the handsome two-storey building which was the CO's house and office combined. There was a good looking, grey-haired woman standing on the second-floor balcony watching the recruits being drilled, and she smiled and waved at Donohue.

Mrs Patterson might only be the wife of the temporary commanding officer, but she was a familiar and popular figure around the fort, and the men relied on her for support when times got tough. They got it, too.

Colonel Patterson was sticking pins in a map when they reported in, and he shook Donohue's hand enthusiastically.

'Not thinking of signing up again, are you, lad? I need a good scout. Heffernan will have told you about Harris? Tragedy, that. I thought there wasn't anything that walked, crawled, bit or stung that could damage that old sidewinder, but it was the water got him in the end. A drink of bad water!'

Donohue for the umpteenth time refused his chance to risk life and sanity by working for pennies in one of the most dangerous places in the Territory, and at long last got a chance to explain what he was there for.

Both commanding officer and NCO gave muffled exclamations of surprise when he mentioned the missing Mexican girl.

'Seen her? We most certainly have seen her! She came through here on her way to Tombstone, a week or so back. Good-looking young lady, too. Didn't like the look of the two men escorting her, or the fact that they were taking her down through the Sulphur Springs road in a wagon, either. Prefer to have seen her on a horse and a damned fast one, too!'

The Sergeant added, 'Most of the lads on the post were delighted to see her come back.'

Donohue was surprised, and for more than one reason. What had the girl and the wagon been doing this far up towards New Mexico? Why had they come down the dangerous Apache Pass? And why did she come back?

He explained his version of the story so far and the fury of Barratt when he had heard Donohue had not brought the girl in with him.

'That's easy enough,' said the officer

triumphantly. 'She wasn't with the wagon because this Barratt man was what she was running away from. She and the wagon came through about five days ago. Three days later she was back, this time with a single escort and on a horse. Nice enough fellow, as well.'

Donohue noticed the sergeant, who had been nodding enthusiastically all through the officer's account, had suddenly stopped nodding and was looking thoughtful. However, he did not interrupt, and Donohue decided to let it drop until he got the NCO by himself, later.

'So you saw her . . . when?' he asked.

The officer cupped his beard in his hands and frowned in an effort to concentrate. Then he jumped up, walked to the door and bellowed, 'Gertrude! Gertude!'

The sound of feet lightly tapping on the stairs, and his wife appeared looking prim.

'Ah, Gertrude, my dear,' said her husband. 'Remember that delightful young Mexican girl who spent the night with us? Donohue here is looking for her. When was she here and how long did she stay?'

'She was here last week,' said his wife crisply, 'came through again with that rather shifty young man three days later, which would make it the day before yesterday, and left with him again yesterday morning. Said they were on their way to Santa Fe – but I think it was just to put us off the track. They went down the pass towards the border. I consider that is more like where they were going.'

Donohue swore mentally. They must have passed

him, a few miles to the north, while he was toiling up the pass and to the fort.

'Why do you want to know, Martin?' asked the colonel's wife. 'What is she to you?'

Donohue told her the whole story, punctuated with muted explosions of disbelief from the colonel, his wife and from Heffernan.

'Started out just as a way of clearing myself of doin' away with the girl I never even met,' he said. 'I came up to find what happened to her, to clear myself. The Earps say they are too busy to get involved, and anyway it's outside their jurisdiction. Sheriff Behan I never met, but his deputies didn't seem inclined to go outside the city limits. Barratt I didn't like even one little bit, and everyone else seemed to be shootin' at me!'

'Who is trying to kill you?' asked the colonel's wife. Of the three of them, she was, characteristically, the one who cut her way through the story to get to the real question.

'Just about everybody, so far as I can calculate,' said Donohue. 'I only got a good look at the back-shootin' ba— man I killed, and I never seen him before in my life.'

'No,' said Mrs Patterson. 'The ones who seem to be trying to kill you are either the ones attached to this Barratt man, or the odd opportunist who attaches himself to them. From the sound of it, I would say you have a price on your head, and this Barratt man is the one who put it there.'

'But that don't make sense! If he wants his bride back in Tombstone, why should he be tryin' to stop the only man lookin' for her?'

She slapped her palm on the table. 'Precisely! But suppose he does *not* want his bride in Tombstone? Suppose what he wants is precisely the opposite?

'You already said people in Tombstone were amazed that he had sent those particular men to bring her back to him. They will be even more surprised that a bride supposedly coming in from Mexico should choose Apache Pass. She must have gone well over a hundred miles out of her way – and been taken through some of the most dangerous territory in Arizona, before she gets to Tombstone.'

He was silent. What she said did make a terrible kind of sense. If Barratt wanted his bride dead, he could not have chosen a better route for killing her. Or, from the sound of it, a better pair of villains.

And if the colonel's wife was right, Barratt's fury at Donohue's intervention was easy to understand. The very worst thing that could happen would be for Donohue to find the Martinez girl alive and well. She might have a very different tale to tell to Tombstone than the official version.

On the other hand, why would Barratt want her dead? If she was the daughter of a rich Mexican rancher, or mine owner, or businessman, she would be an excellent bride for him. Alive, but so far unwed, she was a good catch but only while still alive.

Dead, she was worth nothing until they were married.

Unless, of course, they actually were married already. If the girl were an heiress, her money would pass to her husband on her death. Control of it, assuming they were already secretly married, would already be in her husband's hands.

So he would not need her alive. Would, in fact, be better off if she were already dead.

And so far as Tombstone was concerned, she was.

CHAPTER NINE

He ate in the post bar with Heffernan, and a string of interested NCOs who came to join them, shared their knowledge and went away about their business.

The picture he built up was a puzzling one. The girl had been through twice, once on her way down the pass with Barratt's two men, then with a handsome young man who looked Mexican, with whom she seemed to be on very warm and close terms. They had overnighted at the fort, the girl in complete respectability with the commanding officer's wife, and passed on north towards Santa Fe, or at any rate, that was what the young man had said.

The girl had not seemed to be under pressure. On the contrary, the men Donahue spoke to all inclined towards the opinion that she was very cosy with her escort, who also paid a flattering amount of attention to her.

The whole thing sounded more like an elopement than a kidnapping, but even if the girl was making off of her own accord, it did not solve his problem. The Earps in particular would not settle for less than a live, testifying bride, and without one, Barratt would simply let it be known that Donohue had failed to produce her because she was dead.

One way or another, he had to turn up in Tombstone with a live, visible girl if he expected to get himself off the hook – and if he intended to settle anywhere in the territory, he must get himself off the hook.

But though the soldiers at Fort Bowie were in the main helpful, they would not necessarily stay that way if they thought he was trying to kidnap an unwilling girl from her lover. He had to handle things very discreetly.

And Donohue was the first man to admit that discretion was alien to his Irish blood and his Irish soul.

He bought drinks for the soldiers, drank cold beer sparingly himself, and when the afternoon turned into evening, got himself a mug of coffee and a piece of the bar's surprisingly good apple pie, and went to arrange a bunk in the lines for the night.

The fort was squarely in the throat of the most convenient route through the mountains towards New Mexico, with the Dos Cabezas to the north and the Chiricahuas to the south of it.

Next town of any size – and the expression was relative – was Lordsburg, the stage post and soon to be the railroad centre over the border which turned Arizona Territory into New Mexico. If the young couple were planning to swing north to Santa Fe or Albuquerque, they were choosing a long, hard road.

At this time of year, even the mountains around Silver City were thinking about snow, and to get stranded in the snows up there would be a perilous thing.

He found himself scratching his thoughts absent-mindedly into a map on the ground, and stared at the scratches he had made.

To get to Apache Pass in order to come down it towards the Sulphur Springs Valley, the girl and her escorts would have had to cross the border at Antelope Wells, work their way up through the Animas mountains, and the Pyramids and swing west through Lordsburg and through Apache Pass.

Cochise himself would have had trouble with that route. It took in some of the wildest and most dangerous country in the Territory. To bring a woman that way would have been suicidally stupid. Yet two tough, experienced men had done it and done it with a wagonload of what looked like ranch supplies.

He leaned back and scraped his map out with his boot, then went back into the bunkhouse and stripped down to his long johns, hung his boots upside down on the end of the cot, and rolled into his blankets.

The quiet voices of healthily tired men were the last sounds he heard until he awakened with a jerk in the first grey light of the mountain dawn.

Reveille had not yet been sounded, and he stamped on his boots outside the door, washed in ice-cold water from the barrel outside, and shivered his way into his clothes before walking to the store for breakfast.

He was startled when his loaded plate was banged down in front of him by a handsome Apache woman with thick black braids hanging on her shoulders and smouldering eyes which dared him to remark on her. She did not return his smile when she dropped a knife and fork in front of him; he had the impression she would rather have driven them into his eyes.

The barman from last night watched him tuck into his pile of eggs, bacon and pancakes with amusement. They were very good, and he remarked on them. The man grinned.

'She got a temper like a sore bear with a stubbed toe, but she sure can cook like an angel,' he said.

'Commanding officer happy about her livin' in the Fort?' asked Donohue.

'We come as a set,' the man said. 'You want one you get the other. Been together since she was a young 'un. Every now and again she tries to stab me, but I don't think she's serious about it. She on'y hits one time in three, and it never goes deep.'

Donohue nodded. 'That's OK, then?'

'Sure it is! Mind, you got to remember I'm generally runnin' away at the time, ain't I, my little papoose?'

He made to put his arm around the woman, and she swung at him with her frying pan. His duck was obviously practised, and there was a flicker of amusement in the woman's eyes as she turned back to the stove and started slapping bacon rashers and a couple of steaks in the pan.

Heffernan came in, hung his coat on a hook near the door and stamped his feet several times to warm them.

'Snow soon, I reckon,' he announced, pointed at Donohue's table and pulled out a spare chair to join him.

'I been thinkin',' he said. 'Them two, the Mexes, I don't reckon they're headin' for Santa Fe at all. Seems agin' logic to me. It's a long way, the weather's turnin' foul, so they can't go high, the Apaches are out, and they'll be watchin' the river. Them two, they ain't got nothin' to look forward to up there.'

Donohue had already reached the same conclusion himself, but he waited for the big sergeant to explain his own reasoning.

'No, I reckon they'll strike south for Antelope Wells. That way they can avoid any searchers, get back across the border, and they're back in their own country.'

It made sense. Why plod north in worse weather to Santa Fe which was thousands of feet higher than Apache Pass, when they could strike south to better weather and be on their way home to Mexico? The southern route was no less dangerous, but it was shorter, even if it ran closer to the Chiricahua mountains and therefore the Chiricahua Apaches. Geronimo, off the reservation, might very easily choose to go south through the land he knew the best.

'I reckon you're right, Heff,' he said. 'Who was the last one to see them?'

The big sergeant accepted a loaded plate from the

Apache woman, and demolished a pile of eggs and bacon before answering.

'Me, likely,' he said indistinctly. 'I was doin' my early rounds and they went past me. Two of them, wrapped up warm, on good horses. Packed saddle-bags. She had a striped mackinaw on, and a man's hat. He had one of them fancy Mexican hats on, and he was muffled up good, too.'

He frowned, staring at his plate.

'Funny thing, though, I'd have thought they needed more supplies than they was carryin', even if they wasn't making for Santa Fe. A pack horse at least, if they was heading for Mexico and the places she could come from.'

He shrugged and wiped his plate with a hunk of bread which would have choked a horse.

Donohue glanced at the clock over the bar and saw it was nearly seven in the morning.

'I better get on the trail, then, Heff,' he said. 'I got to head them off before they get to the border, or I'll lose them. The Mexican authorities won't take too kindly to me tryin' to bring a Mexican girl back across the line, particularly if she don't want to come!'

CHAPTER TEN

Even at the fort the weather was cold and blustery, but once he was out of the confines of the pass, the wind really cut in, and Donohue found himself riding with his chin tucked into his collar, and his eyes watering.

He knew that the wind only felt cold by contrast to the usual warmth of the area, but his blood was not used to this, and he rummaged in his saddle-bag for a scarf and was glad to wind it round his neck.

He knew he was following a hunch rather than a clear piece of reasoning, but he had followed such hunches before and not been betrayed.

The longer he rode, the more sure he was that the couple were ahead of him, and the more he was determined to catch up with them before they got to the border.

Trying to track two particular horses in the dry trail, ridden over time after time by patrols, travellers passing through and the various freight wagons and even the stagecoaches, was pointless. In the dust there was no individual imprint to recognize, even if he had been given a chance to examine the prints from these particular horses in isolation, before setting out.

What he needed was something to distinguish these two horses from the hundreds which had passed this way, and he found it.

His first find was a point where two horses had diverged from the trail and ridden up into a defile leading into the hills. It was the first diversion, and the hills around here were no place to wander. After an examination of the trail, he came to the conclusion that the couple he was trailing had indeed done something almost suicidally crazy and put themselves even deeper into Apache territory.

The rocky defile climbed gently away from the trail, towards the east, and the further it went, the narrower it became.

Donohue leaned from the saddle every now and again to look for further tracks and was rewarded from time to time with a scrape mark against the rocky side of the defile where a hoof had slipped, but there was no consistent trail as such.

The horses moved up the trail in single file, with one faint set of hoof prints overlaying the other in the thin dust.

Above him, the walls of the defile closed tighter, until he was riding in a cleft so deep and so narrow that it was filled with a soft, diffused light. The walls were striated tightly with horizontal scoring, as though someone had sand blasted them.

It was a short time before he identified and recognized the noise in the same instant. It was the sound of the powder-fine sand falling in incessant curtains down the walls. His horse's movements dislodged the sand caught in the striations in the side of the canyon, and sent it misting to the ground in almost invisible curtains.

In the drier times of summer he might not have worried about it. But at this time of year, the desert storms could burst elsewhere without warning, and this canyon was clearly a watercourse when the mountains drained off.

He had heard of these before, and a Navajo guide he had camped with over one hellish month of storms and snow some years back had told him of them. The man had described one to be found up near the gigantic cleft in the ground men were beginning to call The Grand Canyon to the north of the Territory. There, they called them 'slot canyons' and stayed well clear of them in any weather.

The hair on the back of his neck prickled as he realized that this twisted and strangely beautiful cleft might at any point become too narrow for the mustang either to carry on or to turn round. The only thing which kept him pushing on was the fact that at least two horses had gone through it ahead of him.

While the sun was still shining outside the cleft, there had been dark clouds to the north and he knew that the narrow, twisting gut of the canyon would fill to the very rim within minutes if there was heavy rainfall in its catchment area. It was the pressure of the sudden flood, which would carry in it pebbles and gravel like a gigantic shotgun charge, which had scoured the canyon out of a rocky cleft.

He breathed a little more easily when they emerged at the top end and he found himself in an expanding basin half filled with tumbleweed. He steered the horse well away from such a convenient hiding place for rattlesnakes.

The tracks he had been following were clearer here, where there was no falling dust to obscure them, and led on up the widening canyon. So far as he knew, and his time at Fort Bowie had given him a chance to get a good general idea of the geography of the area, there was neither town nor transport up here, and they were too far south of Steins for the railroad to be their destination along this route.

So why were they following this road to nowhere?

He found a slight game trail climbing away from the floor of the defile, and urged the mustang up it, watching with pleasure as the tough little horse picked its way up the eyebrow of a trail.

Suddenly and unexpectedly he topped out on the shoulder of a knob of rock and found himself looking down an array of deeply cut narrow canyons angling away into the hills to the north.

Ahead of him and perhaps a mile away along a canyon leading directly north, he could see two figures on loaded horses making their way towards a place where canyons intersected and formed a small playa. There was water down there, and he could see against the far wall of the playa a vast cavern in which a pueblo had been built, like a doll's house in a play-room shelf.

The pueblo had been built, he knew, by the people who had lived here before the Navajo, the Apache and the various smaller tribes who now ranged Arizona and made their homes there.

Today's Indian would not go anywhere near them, never entered the neat apartment buildings tucked into the shallow caves and treated with deep suspicion anybody who did. These days the surprisingly sophisticated blocks were inhabited only by snakes and scorpions and a variety of other wild life which bit, stung or poisoned with enthusiasm.

So he knew where to find his quarry. But what concerned him suddenly even more than them was another group which was moving through the canyons and clefts spread out below him.

The Apaches, possibly even Geronimo and his group, were out and moving south, a direction which could only bring them into contact with the two Mexican figures threading their way through the rocks. He was not certain whether the Indians were yet aware of the other couple, but sooner or later they certainly would be, and the Apaches' hatred for Mexicans was well known. Considering the history of relations between the native Indians and the incoming Spanish slave hunters and bullion raiders, with a sword in one hand and a rosary in the other, the hatred of the Indians first for the Spanish and more recently for the Mexican descendants, the prospect could only be bloody and sickening.

A dead witness was no use to him, so if he wanted her testimony to clear him of suspicion in Tombstone, he had to make sure the girl survived –

even if he were not naturally inclined to save her from the terrible fate which would be hers in the hands of the Apaches.

What her escort was thinking of, bringing her into this situation, he could not imagine, but whatever the man's motive, he had to be stopped.

CHAPTER ELEVEN

Donohue reached into his saddle-bag and brought out a battered pair of binoculars.

They brought the figures of the Mexican couple into sharp focus. The man was leading as he had expected, but what he had not expected was that he was leading the girl's horse on a long rein. The figure of the girl seemed to be uncomfortable in the saddle, and Donohue was not certain even that she was conscious. Her head seemed to be rolling from side to side, and she was slumped in her seat.

He swung the binoculars and picked up the Apaches. There was a group of around thirty of them, all mounted and some encumbered with bundles. The men led the group, which was strung out along a canyon and moving easily and surprisingly fast, with a couple of warriors bringing up the rear. They looked like a tight military formation covering ground at a steady, mile-eating speed without fuss.

In Apache society, the women were responsible for the home and cooking, as well as looking after the children. The men were warriors and hunters, and responsible for the extended family of their wives.

That did not mean that only the men were capable of fighting, of course. Apache women fought like mountain cats, and the Lord help any enemy who fell into their hands. The women reserved a special and inventive cruelty for them, and Mexicans were their special targets.

This particular group seemed to be moving to an established pattern, to know exactly where they were going.

Unfortunately, their target seemed to be the deep valley in which he could see the pueblo, and towards which the Mexicans were hurrying. He could understand that if the Mexican man knew his territory, he could also know about the pueblo, and that it would afford shelter, warmth and relative safety.

The trouble was that at their present gait the man and woman would find it a close run thing to arrive there before the Apaches.

Donohue packed away the field-glasses, and hurried the mustang down into a gully which promised to get him to the cliff dwellings more directly than the Mexican couple and, with any luck, before the Indian party. The sturdy mountain horse tucked its head down, and went off at a fast walk which turned into a lope as the canyon floor levelled out.

What the scout had not counted on was that the Indians had their own scouts out and that those same scouts had seen him. Further down among the rocky clefts, cold black eyes watched him start down into the canyons, and clucked their horses into motion. They might not know what he was aiming at, but they could see which way he was going, and they had time to head him off.

To an Apache warrior a white man was an excellent prize. He was, like an unexplored mine, stuffed with valuable things.

To start with, there would be his weapons. The Indians were rooted in a stone age culture and, until comparatively recently, his axe heads and knife blades had been chipped with infinite patience and skill from flint.

Iron and steel had arrived in their culture along with their most dangerous enemies, when the Spanish explorers started to filter up from Mexico in search of gold and slaves. They expected to take both from the Indians, for early explorers had returned to the Spanish colonies with tales of fabulous cities of gold and jewelled palaces somewhere – the explorers were never exactly certain just where – to the north.

When they found only mystified Indians, they first tried to force the knowledge of the Cities of Gold from them, then to trick it from them. Blood was inevitably spilled, since the Indians did not know what they were talking about, and at first resented and then violently retaliated when torture was tried as a way of prising the knowledge from them.

The lines of battle having been set, both sides applied themselves to the conflict with vigour and increasing skill.

Geronimo, who was a holy man first and foremost

and became a terrifying guerrilla fighter later, was the most ruthless and inventive character in a long line which included Cochise, and a whole line of other fighters.

The two scouts who had picked up Donohue hurried their ponies through the maze of small canyons until they were ready to attack.

They were nonplussed to find that the canyon, in which they had confidently expected to find Donohue, was empty. Puzzled, they cast around for tracks and found none. One dismounted and examined the sandy floor of the defile. Maybe, he thought, the white man had been crafty enough to drag a blanket to cover his tracks.

But they found no scuff marks, no half obliterated tracks, nothing to indicate a rider had passed this way at all. Puzzled and worried, they turned their horses to backtrack. As they did so, one was aware of a sudden movement which should not have been there, over to his right.

He turned his head towards the half perceived threat and the blade of the thrown Bowie knife sank accurately into his left eye socket. The pony, startled, bucked once and unbalanced the suddenly lifeless figure, which rolled backwards over its rump and fell on its heels as it kicked them up to run off.

The body lay in the dusty floor of the canyon and the flurry of dust caused by the animal's flight slowly dissipated on the cold, still air.

Nothing else moved.

After a few seconds, the second warrior came back

to look for the first.

The second scout did not rush up to the body to see if there was any sign of life. He could see from where he was that there was a knife hilt protruding from the eye socket, and he knew that no man survives a knife in the eye.

The knife had remained in the eye, so the thrower had not made any attempt to reclaim it. The second Apache knew the value of a Bowie knife, and if the owner had not reclaimed it, the probability was that he had not so far had a chance.

On the other hand, the Apache did not feel that he was being watched. He would have been hard put to explain why not, but the gut feeling that he was alone with the body refused to go away.

At last, his curiosity proved stronger than his caution, and he allowed the horse to approach the body. Nothing happened, so he swung down and reached out to pull the knife from the eye socket.

He heard the faint but unmistakable scrape of cloth on stone, just in time to throw himself into a forward roll which he turned into a squirming change of direction and threw himself behind a buttress of rock at the side of the trail. A true warrior, he had retained his hold on the carbine, and as he fell into the shelter of the rock, he cocked the weapon and crouched silent for a moment, listening.

Donohue sat behind his own rock and swore bitterly at himself. He had held his fire when he saw the second Apache appear because he did not want to alert the main body which he knew must be coming up not very far behind the scout.

Only pure luck had saved him from the ambush the Apaches had planned. He had taken a slightly more roundabout route to get to this point, because a rock fall had partially blocked the canyon he had originally chosen.

As a result, he arrived in this canyon slightly later than he had intended, in time to see the first Apache tracker searching it for his, Donohue's tracks.

It was a shock for two reasons. The first that he had thought himself unobserved and the second that he had mistaken the advance scout for a member of the main body and, as a result, thought they were between him and the Mexican couple.

He had been about to recover his Bowie when the second Apache appeared, and he was loath to shoot at the Indian in case of alerting the larger group.

Now, he had the worst of all possible worlds. The Apaches knew of his presence, as was made obvious by the activities of the first scout. He had obviously been searching for something he knew should be there, and could not find. Since the man was a native of the territory, that something was most probably Donohue.

When the Apache scout had turned his attention to backtracking up the canyon, Donohue knew he would sooner or later come across the mustang's tracks, and the horse itself. He could not afford to be set afoot so he had killed the man.

Now he dare not leave the live scout behind the rock. At the very least the man could tell the other Indians Donohue was around. At the worst, he could even now be preparing to ambush the white man, and after that the Mexican girl and her escort.

But where were the rest of the Apaches and their women and children?

Donohue watched the rock buttress which hid the warrior carefully. Sooner or later the man had to move, and to move would be to expose himself to a bullet. Donohue had just the bullet ready for him. Sure, it would expose his presence to the Apaches but then, these two proved that the Indians already did know about him, so he had nothing more to lose.

By now, he was getting desperate. All he wanted was for the girl to clear him of the rumour that he had killed her himself. The last thing he wanted was to get involved in a personal struggle against Geronimo and his group. For one thing, people who took on Geronimo tended to end up dead.

As he was working out what to do, he decided to change position in the hope that he might be able to see the Apache behind his rock. Carefully, Donohue eased himself round the foot of his own refuge, staying close to the ground, and scuttled across the canyon floor to the far side, where he dropped behind another rock.

Nothing happened.

He eased his head around the base of the rock until he could see the Apache's refuge. As he had expected, his new position gave him a vantage point from which he could see almost the whole of the recess behind the rock.

It was empty.

Without pausing, Donohue rolled sideways once and then again. A ricocheting bullet gave a banshee scream as he moved, and a second smacked into the canyon wall as he came off the sand running, jinking like a jack-rabbit, back to his original refuge.

Just before he got there, he made a sudden leap to his right, rolled sideways and came to his feet, drawing his Colt as he did so.

The move caught the Apache by surprise as he leaned out from his cover to fire again. Rifle to shoulder, attention on the rock he had been expecting Donohue to use for cover, he was caught flat footed, and the big, soft .44 slug went in under his breastbone and knocked him backwards off his feet. He hit the ground on his shoulder blades and lay still.

Donohue did not wait to check on him. He ran past the first Apache, grabbing his knife as he went, and sprinted to his horse, tucked away in a little bay in the canyon wall, threw himself into the saddle and hit the canyon floor running. No point after that barrage of shots in pretending his presence was a secret any more. In any case the Apache scouts had known where to find him which meant the rest of the Indians did as well.

There was a time to fight and a time to run. This was the time to run, and Donohue ran like a rabbit.

CHAPTER TWELVE

Donohue had been right and he had also been wrong. The first Geronimo and his band knew of the presence of their enemies was the succession of shots from their scout's rifle. They had all heard rifle and pistol shots, and knew the different sounds well.

Usually, it was white men who used the short hand-guns, though Apaches, of course, looted them from the bodies of their enemies. To an Indian, however, a rifle, besides killing enemies, brought down game at impossibly long range. Since the Indians' only source of ammunition was the white man, and the sale of arms and ammunition to Indians was forbidden, few had the resources to learn accuracy at any but point blank range with a handgun.

So a handgun, which made a different sound than a rifle, generally meant white men. The warriors kicked up their horses, and hurried forward along the canyon to where the advance scouts had apparently run into white men.

Bending over the horse's neck, Donohue rattled along the canyon, unsure even of what he might meet around the next corner. The Indians he had run into had been moving up the rocky cleft from the direction of the pueblo canyon, and he expected the main body to be that way, too.

There was a cut-off he had noted from his vantage point, and if he got to it before the Apaches, he could turn aside out of their path and still arrive at the pueblo only a little after the Mexicans.

He reached the turnoff, swerved into it – and found himself facing the interested if disconcerted faces of the Apaches' main body advanced guard as it hurried forward to see the action.

Both sides were surprised, but Donohue was already in motion, and his horse was agile and fast, and it managed both to rear and turn in the same movement, and was instantly racing, belly down and hell for leather back into the main canyon.

Donohue stuck to its back and threw the reins over when they came into the canyon, and the horse turned without a slip and hammered down the trail. Behind him he could hear the shrill yips of the Apaches as they followed him.

The pueblo was standing back from the floor of the canyon, and the approach to it was surprisingly gentle. A seam of rock stood out from the main face of the bottom edge of the recess, and the mustang went up it like a gazelle.

He steered the animal up to the foot of the pueblo's buildings, and into a tumbledown ruin at the side of the main tenement. There had been a gutter along one side of it, and somebody had added a crude wooden partition within the space behind the frontal wall.

In it, there were two horses, looking over their shoulders at him, and champing on a bait of grass which had been left there

Startled, he dropped from the saddle and added his own horse to the line. Being a desert horse and used to fending for itself, it immediately started munching on the feed provided.

Where there were horses, there were riders, and the only pair of riders Donohue knew of in the area were the Mexicans, so he hitched the mustang, dragged his rifle out of the saddle boot and started cautiously for the climbing holes he could see in the canyon wall alongside the wall of the pueblo.

Halfway up, he emerged from the shelter of the improvised stable wall and was greeted with a chorus of yells from the canyon behind him. A bullet raised a puff of dust from the rock above him, and howled off into space.

He wanted to get inside the walls, but the horses' owners, crouching within and hearing the Apaches' whoops and the firing, would certainly fire on the first human being to come jumping over the wall. He had better reassure them.

'*Hola!*' he shouted at the occupants of the ruins above him. '*Se puede entrar?*'

There was no response from the ruin, and in a spatter of firing, another bullet smacked into the wall, this time much closer. He repeated the greeting but without response, and finally hauled himself up to the flat roof of the ruin and dropped down into the dark interior.

Outside, the howls of the Apaches took on a disappointed note, and he wondered how long it would be before their desire to kill him overcame their religious conviction that the ruins should be left alone. Any Indian who entered the abode of the dead, he knew, had to go through a long and irksome series of ceremonies to purify himself afterwards.

For the moment, though, those inside the ruin were safe from those outside it. He found a former window in the outside wall and peeped out cautiously. A bullet instantly chipped the stone by his face and a shower of stone splinters rattled on his hat.

His eyes were becoming accustomed to the dim light inside the ruin, and, staying well away from corners and deep recesses where the creatures of the dark may be hiding, explored as much as he could.

The room he had entered was empty of any kind of furniture, which was hardly surprising, but there were some broken pots in a recess in the wall. He struck a match to see them and wondered at the intricate decorations on the surviving pieces.

He had seen such shards before, and knew that although they assumed a secretive and knowing look when asked about them, the Indians now living in the territory knew almost as little about their origin as the white incomers.

There was nothing else in the room, so he ducked through a low archway and into the next building.

The girl he had been hunting was lying against the wall, wrapped in blankets and motionless. His heart sank at the thought that after all the trouble he had taken to find her, she might even be dead.

But he struck a match and lighted a stub of candle from his pocket to see her properly and was relieved to see her eyelids flicker. She took a deep breath and moaned a little but did not awaken, even when he shook her shoulder gently.

He held the candle closer, and was struck by the girl's beauty. Until now, he had simply thought of her as a Mexican girl, olive-skinned and dark haired, with liquid eyes and a plump body.

This girl, however, was remarkable. Her skin was lightly tanned, her hair was black enough, but lustrous and heavy like swags of silk. The lashes which lay on her slightly flushed cheeks were long, thick and dark.

She was remarkable. And she was unconscious, and alone in an apparently deserted ruin.

He raised the light and looked around. There were some saddle-bags in the corner, and a lantern hung, unlit, from a peg driven into the wall. In the flickering light of the candle, he could see that this part of the ruin at any rate, had been turned into something like a camp.

There were ashes in a neat fireplace near a cleft in the cliff which formed the back wall of the room, and smoke stains around the crack told him it worked as a chimney. Near it, another niche, half natural but deepened and levelled by human hand, was being used as a pantry. There were some cans of food and a stone jar which contained on inspection, beans, a sack of coffee beans, and a couple of tin plates.

He searched the rest of the room and found steps

hacked out of natural holes in the cliff face which led upwards and through a trap in the ceiling.

The girl stirred and muttered but refused to respond to his gentle shaking, and he did not want to try anything more vigorous because she was easier to deal with asleep than awake, for the moment. In any case, if her increased restlessness was anything to go by, she was in the process of awakening naturally.

He clambered up the hole ladder and found himself looking along a deep ledge which formed a path along the back of the cavern which contained the cliff dwellings. It had been covered over the years with a layer of dust in which footprints of a man in high heeled boots could clearly be seen. They showed that the ledge had been used several times to come and go, and the latest line of prints, clear cut and crisp, led away towards the end of the cavern.

He thought of returning to the building and questioning the girl when she woke up, but if, as seemed likely to him, she had been only semi conscious when she was brought here, it was unlikely she would know any more than he did.

The Indians outside seemed to have fallen surprisingly quiet and he walked along the outside wall of the ruin until he could see down into the canyon. To his surprise, only two of the warriors were in sight, sitting on their heels in the shade of the far side of the little amphitheatre formed by the intersection of the two canyons.

One of them noticed the movement within the cavern, and threw a bullet his way, the report sounding curiously flat as though the sound was muffled by

94

the cave. The bullet came nowhere near him and he ignored it.

However, the report had apparently roused the girl, for he heard her call out: 'Luis?'

He walked back along the top of the wall and dropped through the trap to the floor of the building, to find her still lying in the blankets, and staring at him, wide-eyed in the gloom. His stub of candle had almost burned away, and he found the lantern from its hook and used the final guttering flame to light it, before the candle finally died.

The golden light of the lantern brought the room into life, and the girl stared round her and at him, then cowered back as he leaned over her, only to give a sharp grunt of disgust as he flicked a scorpion from her blanket and stamped on it.

'Make sure there aren't any more in the blankets,' he told her, and smothered a grin as she shot out of the cocoon of wrappings and across the room.

He picked up the blankets one by one in his gloved hands and shook them, but nothing deadly fell out, and he folded them neatly and tucked them on top of the stores.

The girl stayed against the wall, watching him with careful eyes.

'*Señorita*,' he said, 'I must ask you not to make a noise. There are Apaches outside, and so far as I know, they are not aware that you are here. At the moment, they are staying outside through their own superstitious beliefs, but anything could break the hold of that belief at any time, and the presence of a woman could very easily change their minds.'

She nodded without speaking, and he knew she understood what he had said, and its implications.

'Where is the man who brought you here?'

She shrugged, and the motion made the jacket, thrown around her shoulders, slip off on one side, showing she was wearing under it a man's woollen shirt, and a leather vest held together at the front with a leather thong and plain bone button. She was also wearing a leather riding skirt, divided so that she could sit astride, and riding boots.

'Luis, the man who brought you here! Where is he?'

She was watching him with a totally expressionless face, and an unreadable expression in her eyes. The lack of any kind of reaction puzzled him. This girl had been brought here apparently while unconscious, awakened by gunshots, to find herself in an abandoned ruin with a total stranger bending over her, and no sign of her friend.

Surely she should be showing something, if only understandable fear.

'*Señorita,*' he said, desperately, 'please say somethin' to show me you understand what's goin' on here. I need to get you away from here somewheres safe! Geronimo is off the reservation with a whole passel o' people, and I believe that the Apaches waiting outside are a part of that band.'

'They are!' she said. Her voice was surprisingly deep for a woman, and musical.

'How come you know?' he asked. 'I thought you was only semi-conscious when you come here, and the Apaches didn't show up until you was already in here. I seen you and I seen them.'

'So?' she spat with sudden venom. 'You spy! You sneak and you spy! You are like all *gringos*. There is no trusting you. You come to steal me away from my friends and sell me to the man who calls himself my husband.'

She stopped suddenly as though she had said something she should not have, and her venomous stare wavered for a moment.

He frowned and repeated, puzzled, 'Your husband? I thought you weren't married yet?' A sudden thought shook him. Suppose he had been following the wrong woman, and the witness he had been seeking was even now riding away to Santa Fe, and far beyond his grasp.

'You are Ysabella Martinez? You are engaged to Lexington Barratt? You were on your way to Tombstone to marry him?'

'No! I am not Ysabella Martinez!' she snapped. '*Dios*! How I wish I were.'

'Then who in creation are you?' he asked. 'I been trackin' Ysabella Martinez for days, and her tracks led right here. You got to be her! There ain't two beautiful Mexican girls in these here hills, for sure!'

She should have picked up on his puzzlement, but she was too overwrought.

'I am Ysabella Barratt! Ysabella Barratt! *Nombre de Dios*! Do you not understand? I am married to that man. Married! Me, who could have taken her pick of the best families in Mexico! Sold off like a house slave to a *gringo* with the manners of a pig! Oh. . .'

At this point English words failed her and she fell

into a torrent of border Spanish which honestly shocked Donohue with its passion and its profanity. He listened with something bordering on awe as she categorized Lexington Barratt's parentage, personal habits, lack of cleanliness and general swinishness.

When she paused for breath, he said, 'Yeah, I know. But why did you marry him in the name o' all that's Holy? He says you are just engaged and he's layin' on a big shindig in Tombstone for your marriage.'

'*Puerco!*' She fairly spat the word. 'The pig may have gone through the ceremony with me, but we shall never lie in the same bed! I will. . . .' The ensuing Spanish was so anatomically detailed that Donohue was again genuinely shocked.

He stopped the flood with a raised hand. 'So why did you marry him? I don't get it.'

She opened her mouth to answer, but a rifle crack from outside broke into their consciousness, and a bullet smacked into the roof of the cave far above their heads.

CHAPTER THIRTEEN

The man in the fancy leather jacket and the big, floppy sombrero was visibly hopping mad. He was a handsome young man, wide in the shoulder and narrow in the hip with trousers which fitted like a second skin down to the knee and flared out to hang over his hand-tooled boots. Round his hips he wore a gun-belt strangely at odds with his fancy *hidalgo* costume for it was well worn and businesslike. The holster was cut away, and the tip of it tied down to his thigh so that the gun remained permanently by his hand when it hung at his side.

The retaining loop of thong had been slipped from the hammer spur so that the gun was ready for a quick draw.

Donohue had seen rigs like that before and they always belonged to men who relied on their gun not just for their lives but for their livelihood. This was a gunman, professional and practised. A man who made his living with his expertise, and sold his skills for high fees.

He was a killer, a hired gun, and what he was doing

in this setting, talking to Apaches who were already on the warpath, Donohue could not guess.

The man was standing on the little rock shelf on which the ramshackle stable had been erected. He had a rifle in his hands, and he was peering up at the pueblo, trying to see who might be peering out.

Down in the floor of the canyon itself, a half-a-dozen Apache warriors were sitting their horses and watching the scene above them. None made any attempt to join in the confrontation, and when Donohue peered down at their faces, he thought he could discern amusement in them.

Two white men about to fight one another? Better than a cabaret for the Indians, and they were relaxed and enjoying themselves.

But why were they here at all, and why were they not firing at the Mexican? Apaches carried a special hatred for the Spanish men who had enslaved them and stolen their women for centuries. Why was this man still alive? Even more interesting, where had he been for the past hours and how had he survived in a canyon full of Apaches who were already on the run from the reservation?

There was no profit in exposing his body to the fire of the Mexican man and possibly the Indians, so Donohue stayed where he was and checked that the magazine of the Winchester was fully loaded. He had a feeling he was going to need every cartridge he had.

Behind him the girl clambered up the ladder and leaned over the edge of the pueblo to peer down. She grinned when she saw her former companion standing below, and shouted: '*Hola, Luis!*' before Donohue could stop her.

The man stepped back so that he could see her better, and waved enthusiastically.

Donohue had not told the girl that he spoke Frontier Spanish, so he kept his face expressionless as the couple talked.

'Ysabella?' called the young man. 'Ysabella, whose is this horse in the stable with those of ours?'

'A man sent by my pig of a husband to take me to his sty in Tombstone!' she replied, with a sideways glance at Donohue to see if he understood. He frowned and looked puzzled.

'Is it that he understands Spanish?' called Luis, guardedly. She assured him that Donohue did not, the contempt dripping from her voice. He was too stupid, she elaborated with what seemed more than necessary scorn. Donohue assumed, accurately, that he was not going to like this conversation.

After that, the questions came thick and fast and the answers rattled off without pause.

Yes, she was feeling better now. The effects of the herb they had inadvertently eaten had almost completely worn off. How was he feeling?

Luis assured her that the Indians had given him a herbal antidote to the 'sleeping weed' they had both eaten, and he now felt fine, He had brought some back for her, but clearly she no longer needed it.

It was at this point that the faintest wrinkle of unease appeared on her face, only to be smoothed away immediately. Donohue who had seen Luis riding perfectly well while the girl was swaying in the saddle, presumably stupefied with the drug she had eaten, wondered if a tiny flicker of suspicion had been born in her mind.

What did he want her to do? she asked. She was sure the toad sent by her husband would be easy to outwit. He was a stupid man with only muscle between his ears.

'Have you a weapon?' asked Luis, easily.

She had. A stiletto in her boot. Did he want her to kill the fool?

Luis quite obviously did, but one of the Apaches was showing more than ordinary interest in the exchange, and even Luis noticed it, and became guarded.

Could she perhaps distract the interloper's attention in some other way while Luis climbed into the ruins and disposed of him?

'What way?' Her voice had changed from cautious to frosty. She was a jump ahead of him, and Donohue was two jumps ahead of her.

'Just distract him while I get up through the ruins. We can talk better when I am in there with you!' Luis for the first time was showing signs of strain. Donohue did not blame him. With a bunch of Apaches covering his retreat one way and an unknown gunman heading him off in the other, Donohue would have been feeling the strain, too.

In fact, he was. Whatever restrictions applied to Luis also applied to Donohue, and nothing about this situation was to his liking.

He was considering whether to cut down Luis where he stood, which was an alternative which became more attractive with every word the man said, or to shoot a couple of the Apache warriors, which would certainly get things moving, but would leave him trapped in these ruins with a girl who was planning on stabbing him to death, and her man who wanted nothing better.

Even if he did get out he would need to outrun a group of Apaches who undoubtedly knew these canyons better than he did, and who were already furious about the scouts he had killed back there in the race to get here.

The girl and Luis had been prattling on in increasingly guarded terms while he planned desperately to get her away from here and back to Earp in Tombstone. It was his only way out of his present fix, but from the terms in which she had spoken of him to Luis, he certainly did not have a chance of persuading her to do it of her own free will.

Absently, he stared behind him and ran his eyes for the umpteenth time over the sides and ceiling of the recess in which the pueblo was built. The rocks were streaked with the curious glassy patina called 'desert glaze'. The stuff seemed to build up on the canyon walls for no particular reason, and it was like some kind of glass which had been spilled on the rock when liquid and then set harder than the rock itself.

It was particularly ironic that it should have spread over the rock where it leaned backwards into the face of the canyon wall, and not where the wall occasionally folded outwards to form a convex surface. Idly, while listening to the increasingly animated argument between the girl and the young man, his eyes followed the unglazed surface upwards to the lip of the canyon.

It was almost as though somebody had deliberately cleaned the glaze off the face of that particular rib, leaving the pitted face of the naked rock.

The very pitted face. His eyes suddenly focused more closely on the rock. There seemed to be some sort of pattern to the pitting on that particular rib. Curious holes abounded on desert cliffs formed by weather damage to the rock. The oddly regular shaped holes formed on the face of the precipices, which, scoured by weather action, left shallow circular pits like a skin disease in the rock face. The ancient ones used them as ladders, and often improved their lay-out to make climbing easier and the people who had built the pueblos in the canyons used them as an escape route.

Could that strangely regular pattern on the rib of the cliff he was staring at possibly be an escape ladder?

The conversation beside him had reached a crescendo. They were arguing now about precisely when Luis would come back to rescue her if she were to stab Donohue to death. Luis had finally become exasperated enough to shout at her.

'Make him to go in the back of the ruins!' he bellowed, much to the amusement of the Apaches below who were now laughing at him openly. 'Make him to go back in the ruins and keep his attention! How? How do I know? Take off your clothes, if all else fails! He is a *gringo*! He is stupid enough to forget everything but his trousers!'

By now, the Apaches were whooping with laughter, and beginning to shout suggestions of their own. They at least could see the funny side of it, Donohue thought. He also thought he was more likely to get a stiletto between his ribs than a soft word and a melting eye, and if Luis kept up with his suggestions, he suspected Luis might also be in line for the stiletto treatment.

The girl had turned to look at him and her eye had a certain calculating quality about it that made him very nervous indeed. Clearly she was considering Luis's suggestion seriously, and that calculation combined with the stiletto in her boot boded ill for Donohue.

If he was not very careful indeed, there would be no point in working out how to get her back to Tombstone. Because he would not survive to get there himself.

His planning was interrupted by the arrival of another Apache warrior in a swirl of dust and on a sweating horse. The man pulled his horse onto its haunches and barked out a message. Donohue was too far away to hear what was said, but the effect on the Apaches was immediate.

The other warriors suddenly lost their sense of humour, and all signs of amusement was washed out of their faces. One of them asked a question, and the newcomer snapped an answer and gestured with his hand, pointing back up the canyon.

Instantly, the Indians pulled their own ponies

around and headed back up the canyon where they had left their families. One of them looked back over his shoulder and threw a shot at the Mexican. He missed, but the bullet spattered him with stone, and he threw himself flat on the shelf outside the stable, and out of sight of the Apache, who geatured scornfully and followed his friends up the canyon.

The truce there had been between Luis and the Indians was clearly over. Whatever the Indians expected to get from the Mexican no longer mattered to them, and they were more concerned with leaving than trading.

Donohue had postponed wondering about the reason the Apaches, who were after all on the run from the army, would have for breaking their journey to meet one of the hated Mexicans. There had clearly been some form of negotiation in progress, abandoned once their families were in danger.

The only thing which would put the families of this particular group in danger was the United States' Cavalry.

It was followed by the faint popping of shots being exchanged, and Donohue concentrated on counting the shots, and for a split second forgot that he was now alone in the ruins with a man who was on negotiating terms with Geronimo and a young woman who had a stiletto in her boot.

He remembered just as the girl's boot scraped on stone, and he heard her grunt with effort. Too late to do anything but let go of his handhold, he fell backwards into the ruin. For just a split second he actually saw a streak of silver moving across his face, which he later realized was the sharp edge of the stiletto blade, then hit the pile of blankets on the rock floor with his shoulders.

It was a fall of over six feet and the blankets were not thick, so the impact hurt and for a second his head swam. As it did so, the girl jumped from the ladder and landed next to him. In the jump, the blade was jarred out of her hand, and he heard it tinkle on the rock floor near his head.

Instinctively, he rolled away from her, and heard her sobbing with rage as she scrabbled among the mess on the floor, looking for it. Since she did not take her eyes off him, the search took her longer than it should have and he had time to catch himself and sit up, grabbing for his gun.

He had not seen or heard anything of her companion, and the man had momentarily slipped to the back of his mind until he heard the rattle of hoofs from outside, and the sound diminishing as the horses got further away.

Donohue was looking at the girl as he heard the horses, and he could see the change of expression on her face. First, exultation as she thought it was her lover coming to rescue her, then confusion as the sound diminished, and changed from rattling to thudding as the horses reached the canyon floor, and finally the pounding as they picked up speed and faded into the distance.

'Luis!' she called. Then, 'Luis! Answer me!'

Only the echo of her own voice answered her, and slowly, unwillingly, her eyes came back to meet Donohue's. For a moment he actually felt sorry for her, then he recalled that she had been looking for her knife to kill him, and he had no idea whether she had found it or not.

'Luis?' she called again, but there was no conviction in her voice.

'He went, girl! He's makin' for the border, at a guess, and he's got three mounts to get him there, so he'll be travellin' fast! What you and I have to think about, now, is how to get to the cavalry without Geronimo findin' us!'

That lit the fire in her eyes again, and she spat on the ground between them.

'Geronimo has no terrors for me! Luis is a friend of him! I am safe with the Apache – but you? You are their enemy! For me they will come back; for you, who would bother?'

He could see the knife, now. It was half concealed by the blanket on which she was kneeling, and its haft stuck out a long reach behind her. To keep her attention so she would no look round, he kept talking as he stood up.

'Strange friends he keeps, your Luis,' he said. 'When he is in trouble they stand back and laugh at him! And when the blue shirts come, they ride away. One of them even shot at him as they went!'

Her eyes wavered a little, so she had not missed the gunfire as they went.

'You are made of lies! They were shooting at you!'

He grinned. 'Sure they were! Apaches are always bad shots. They can afford to spray slugs all over the landscape!'

She knew enough about Indians to realize that this

108

was a nonsense. Men who must buy every bullet with blood had to be good shots, and the Apache warriors were better than most cavalrymen. In any case, the retreating warriors could not have seen Donohue from their horses, while they could clearly see Luis.

If they were shooting at Luis, they were not the friends he claimed. Apaches did not make friends with Mexicans, whom they identified with the Spanish colonizers and slave traders, and fit for nothing but prolonged torture and death in inventive ways.

'If I was Luis, I'd be off like a jack-rabbit and I wouldn't stop this side o' the border!' Donohue pressed on relentlessly. 'At the moment, he ain't got no girl to trade, he held up Geronimo before he could get out o' the country, and if I'm right and that was General Crook them scouts was shoutin' about, he's got both the cavalry and the Indians on his tail!'

She spat contempt at him, but there was a worried crease in her forehead, and the contempt was not as deeply entrenched as it had been before. Also, Luis had gone and there was no sign of him coming back.

'Why was you pretty well unconscious in the saddle when you come here? You was swayin' around like a tree in a gale,' he said.

'Pah! How do you know how I was riding?' she said. But there was an edge of worry in her voice.

'I could see you from back up there on the rim,' he said. 'I thought you was tied to the saddle, and five gets you ten you never saw the road up here.'

She was beginning to worry about her position, and he pressed on.

109

'Don't make no never mind,' he said. 'Facts are facts, and the fact is that we are here alone, only the Apache and your absent swain know we're here, and neither of them wishes us well. We have to get out of here, and we have to go now!'

He leaned forward and started to pick up the blankets and shake them out carefully. In the process, he managed to palm the stiletto and slipped it into his own boot. The sharp point and blade made him nervous, but a knife in the hands of this hot blooded Mexican with a temper like a mountain cat, made him more so.

After a moment, she started to help, holding the blankets at arm's length and keeping herself well back. The scorpion had clearly not been forgotten. He noticed her searching the floor carefully as she did so, and knew she was looking for the knife.

It was going to be a long, tense walk if he had to guard himself against both Apaches and the girl, and he was not going to sleep much or well.

He rolled the blankets into two packs, tied them with twine from his pocket, and handed her one.

She stared at the roll with scorn and made no attempt to take it.

'I am not a pack animal!' she said haughtily.

'I dunno what kind o' animal you are now, but I tell you this, *señora*,' he said, 'if you don't carry your own blankets, from tonight you are goin' to be a real cold animal!'

CHAPTER
FOURTEEN

The lieutenant in charge of the cavalry patrol hunkered down by his Apache tracker and listened intently while the man explained what he had found. From time to time, the Apache turned over a pebble or a lump of compacted dirt to demonstrate what he was talking about, and the lieutenant examined it carefully and tried to memorize it for future reference.

Just here, two canyons joined, in a rough letter Y, the one he was following from the north, ahead of Crook and his main body, and the one which came in from the east, and out of which came a river of tracks turning south towards the border and Mexico.

Lieutenant Michael Benetto was a graduate of West Point and had arrived in Arizona only a year before, sparkling with new bars and insignia, and bursting with military method and brass-bound correctness. He had, in fact, been a casualty waiting to happen.

All his new bravado disappeared with dramatic speed in the space of a single cavalry patrol along the Mogollon Rim, when he was ambushed, lost five men in the first burst of fire, and managed to get the rest of them out only by being as brutal and as fast-moving as his enemy.

From the military point of view the patrol had been a disaster; from Benetto's point of view, it was a brutal, bloody lesson in guerrilla tactics and he learned it well.

Crook was a hard taskmaster, but a true expert in his chosen profession of arms. He was a veteran of the War Between the States, of which he had heartily disapproved, and from which he had learned a great deal.

The most important among those lessons was the one which said he should throw away the military rule book and study the successful tactics of his enemies in terrain which they knew and he did not.

In Arizona, he quickly realized how the Indians, and in particular the Apache were able to run rings around the cavalry sent to control them.

The weight of equipment required by regulations to be carried by each trooper was so great that the individual troopers were weighed down by it all; in this unforgiving terrain some items – rations among them – had to be carried in wagons with each column.

Arizona was not a countryside built for wagons. Too much of the terrain was standing on one edge, the general observed, and the Indians – the Apache prominent among them – recognized this, and took advantage of it.

When large army detachments were sent in pursuit of them, the Apaches took to the hills, where the defiles were narrow, the trails, observed one civilian scout, 'rough as a bear's ass'. The Apaches had long realized that all they had to do was retreat into the maze of narrow, steep canyons, and leave the cavalry and its wagons to plod along behind, until it could get no further.

The Indians were stunned when Crook, having watched his quarry disappear into the canyons, abandoned his wagons, put his mountain guns and his supplies onto mules, and followed right along behind them.

Suddenly, the deal was changed. The Indians could no longer evade their pursuers simply by going into places the army could not.

Crook had long used common sense rather than regulations, and took to a mule himself instead of a charger, carried a shotgun instead of a rifle, and even abandoned formal uniform for more comfortable civilian dress.

On Lieutenant Benetto's first patrol, the young man had turned out as if for parade at West Point, his brasses shining, his kepi pulled down level with his eyes, his sabre rattling gently in its metal scabbard, and his tunic buttoned up to the neck. The temperature was just over a hundred in the shade, and the sun was falling on his neck like a hammer.

The soldiers and the Apache scouts regarded him with mixed emotions. They all found him funny, which was to be expected with an unfledged officer, but they also felt alarm that this officer would be in charge of their patrol.

To the Tonto Apaches, one blue-bellied soldier looked very much like another, and they all looked like large, slow-moving targets. The war party which picked up Benetto's patrol satisfyingly far from the fort fell on it like a pack of wolves, isolated it in a box canyon against the Mogollon Rim, and settled down for a long gun battle.

The first thing the lieutenant did was to establish a perimeter, and the second was to secure his horses at the back of the canyon. He had already lost a number of his patrol at the first attack, and he could see the bodies lying out in the open.

One of the men was not dead, and the Apache warriors took to shooting into him to try and get the troopers within the perimeter to mount a rescue bid.

Lieutenant Benetto, outraged at these tactics, ran out to the wounded man, humped him over his own back and ran back to the perimeter. Though the man was far gone, and died later, the young officer had established a principle he went on to practise all his military career, which was that none of the men under his command was ever abandoned to the enemy.

The men warmed to him and the scouts grunted their approval. After that, one of the scouts brought him a wide-brimmed patrol hat from one of the dead men, and he abandoned his kepi, put on the prof-fered felt hat, and wore it, or at any rate, one like it, for the remainder of his career.

Today, he was seeking the tracks of Geronimo's

fleeing band, with a detachment at his back and an Apache scout at his side. Another, smaller patrol had branched off further north to follow a second trail into the canyons, and it looked as though they had found him or at least his tracks.

The scout crouched by the tracks on the canyon floor, and began pointing out characteristics. In the soft sand it was not easy, because a horse's hoof merely left a funnel shaped indentation, and no characteristics appeared. In one canyon junction, however, there had been a seep which kept the canyon damp, and the ground took a print. What attracted the scout's attention was that there had been a number of Indian ponies, stepping sprightly, and their tracks were overlaid by those of a number of shod horses.

'White men follow patrol. Patrol follow Apache,' he opined. Benetto nodded, examining the tracks carefully.

'How many you reckon?' he asked. The Indian stared at the tracks and shrugged.

'Apaches six hands,' he said. 'Not all warriors. Some ponies carry light. Women and children. Geronimo.'

Benetto nodded. Somewhere ahead, there was also an army patrol which was hanging on Geronimo's heels and by this time needed support.

'Blue-bellies follow Apaches. Same number horses. No dead.'

Benetto nodded. That would be Lieutenant Pritchard who had branched off further north to cover another route through the canyons.

'Three horses follow blue bellies, close behind!'

Almost treading on Pritchard's heels. Who were they?

He was standing up to stretch his back when the tracker gave a surprised grunt and leaned forward over the tracks. Benetto bent his back again, to see what the man had found.

'Man and woman,' said the scout. 'On foot. Follow white men's horses. Not long.'

So there was a man and a woman ahead of them, too. And they had passed since the Indians and the three white men on their horses.

'Regular parade!' he said drily. 'Reckon we better join 'em, Victorio. Lead on!'

What in the name of tarnation was a woman doing in these canyons at a time like this? And on foot? For some reason the picture of the Mexican lady who had called at the fort slipped into his mind.

He stopped in the act of mounting his horse, and dropped back to the ground, leaning over the tracks the Apache had found.

The woman's tracks were easy to find, since they had been made after all the others. She had a small, well-shaped boot and an easy stride. He wondered.

'Victorio! You seen these prints before?'

The Apache did not bother to get down to the trail again. He nodded, impassive.

'Where?'

'At fort. Mexicana ride through two, three days ago. Those horses' – he pointed at the trail of the shod horses – 'those horses also. Mexicano man, Mexicana woman, scout Donohue. All three follow

Geronimo. Maybe only horses.'

Benetto thought the same. The man and the woman had been set on foot by the rider with three horses. They followed behind to try and recover their mounts, perhaps. They may even know about the cavalry force ahead of them and be trying to join it.

Whichever was happening, they were now between him and his goal, and he could pick them up and perform his duty at the same time. At any rate, Crook, coming down with the main column, would need to know of their presence. He detached a man to ride back and deliver the message, as well as updating his own report.

It was time to pursue the fleeing Apaches and bring them back to the reservation before they had time to spread any more bloody chaos.

He raised one gloved hand above his head and waved the patrol forward.

CHAPTER FIFTEEN

Donohue pulled the girl behind a rock for the umpteenth time, ignoring her indignant protest. He was getting used to them and even the almost unbearable temptation to smack her every time she opened her mouth was fading away.

They stood behind a rock while the hammering hoofs he could hear got closer, and only stepped out when he realized the man galloping up the canyon was a soldier. The cavalryman hauled his horse to a dramatic standstill, which threw a cloud of dust and small stones all over Donohue, and swore excitedly, stopping instantly when he realized that one of the two people standing in the trail was a woman.

'Hello, Howie!' said Donohue. 'Where's th column?'

'Donohue!' exclaimed the rider. 'Where d'you spring from? I heard you was at the fort!'

'I come from just down the side canyon. Yes I was at the fort. Where in tarnation's that column at?' repeated Donohue He was getting very short of patience, and walking for some miles in his high heeled riding boots dragging a sulky, unco-operative woman behind him was taking a heavy toll on what patience he had left.

'Column's behind you, and the general's with it,' the rider supplied in fast, staccato tones. 'Don't I get to meet the lady? Never had a chance at the fort.'

'Señorita – sorry, Señora – Ysabella Barratt,' said Donohue. The girl's explosion of indignation was stilled when she saw the expression on his face.

'Barratt? Like the Barratt in Tombstone?' asked the trooper.

'Yup!'

'But he says she's dead!' Howe protested. 'Come over the wires this mornin'. Killed on the trail to Tombstone by. . . .'

He stopped when he realized he was talking not only to the 'dead' woman but also to her alleged murderer.

'Yeah,' said Donohue. 'See why I have to get her back to Tombstone?'

'Sure do! But why not take her to the General? He'll put things right with the law for you.'

'First, I got to find our horses, and then I got to show her in Tombstone. Good idea about Crook, though. I can show her to him on the way.'

'Better be quick,' said Howe. 'He'll be out over the border by tonight. I was just sent up from the advance guard to tell him the Indians are headin' for the line hell bent for leather! Once they're over, they're goin' to disappear faster'n a beer on payday!'

He glanced up the canyon and his face suddenly straightened.

'Hell's teeth! Here's the advance guard now. I got to report to Lieutenant Benetto right away.'

He spurred up the canyon and Donohue saw him pull up in front of the column in another cloud of dust.

He and the woman stayed where they were until a couple of troopers trotted down to the them, and helped them up onto their own horses. Donohue noticed that he was riding on the horse's rump while Ysabella was helped into the saddle and the trooper sat behind her. This made it necessary for him to put his arms around the girl, and the expression on his face made it clear that the process did not upset him one little bit.

Ysabella snatched a look at Donohue which had doubt written all over it, but she had heard and understood the implications of what Howe had said, and the fact was clearly making her re-think the situation.

They rode back to the advance guard where Benetto greeted Donohue by name and listened to his story carefully.

His eyebrows knitted when he heard about Luis and his claims that Ysabella would be safe with the Apaches.

'Safe? She'll be a slave or dead,' he snapped. His sergeant, riding alongside, nodded his agreement. He had seen some of the women who had been betrayed to the Apaches. They were not a pretty sight.

'Anybody like to profit from it, if you were to disappear, ma'am?' he asked, abruptly.

Ysabella flashed him a resentful look, but eventually had to admit that she could think of at least one good reason several people might greet her disappearance without mourning.

'There's something funny about the Tombstone situation, too, Lieutenant,' said Donohue. 'This man Barratt has told the town that he is expectin' Señorita Martinez in town to celebrate their weddin'.'

Benetto allowed that the man who married her would surely have plenty to celebrate, and Donohue was amazed to see the girl blush.

'But if they're married already, why tell the folks in town she's comin' to Tombstone for a wedding?' said Benetto.

'And why take her to Tombstone, which is only a few miles north of the border, by takin' her through Apache Pass and down Sulphur Springs Canyon?' said Donohue.

'Don't make sense. That's a dangerous road, best o' time, and now Geronimo's on the prod again, it's worse than ever.'

'Why, that's how I got involved in this mess! The men who was sent to bring her home to her lovin' groom was ambushed there. I buried them myself.'

That did hit home with the girl. She twisted in the saddle to stare at him.

'Buried them? They are dead?' she said.

'Only thing to do with dead men, *señora*, and Adam ain't no deader!'

'*Por Dios*!' she swore, and was about to say more when the scout who had been ahead of the patrol came into sight, riding fast and leading two horses. They were the missing mounts, and Donohue and the girl remounted to the obvious disappointment of the trooper whose horse she had been sharing. The lieutenant's smothered grin said he had not missed the reaction.

The scout explained that he had come across the horses running loose further down the canyon, and gathered them in. He guessed they were the missing mounts of the couple he had seen join the patrol. No, he had not seen another rider with them, and there had been no tracks to indicate anybody else had been there.

He was himself an Apache, and if he said he had seen no tracks, there were no tracks to be seen. Donohue began to wonder about Luis. From the look on her already thoughtful face, so did the girl.

Benetto might have been a sympathetic ear, but he was also a working soldier on an important assignment. He did not need civilians tacked onto his responsibilities, and he made it quite clear.

'Trail behind us is clear right back to the column,' he told Donohue. 'We scouted it and I'll vouch for it. Any hostiles are right out there in front of us, and we saw no signs any had broken off from the party. Should be safe for you to take the Señorita Martinez . . . er, Señora Barratt . . . back as far as the fort, at least. You can speak to the General on the way, and he'll vouch for you when you need him.

'But get him now, or he'll be over the border and out o' touch, maybe for weeks.'

Donohue raised a hand in farewell, and led the

way back up the valley to the cloud of dust which indicated the main column, and General Crook.

A couple of hours later, they were on their way north again, this time with the general's signed letter that he had met Señorita Martinez/Señora Barratt and was satisfied that the young woman he had seen was alive, well, unhurt and not under pressure to give false witness.

'Best I can do under the circumstances,' he said apologetically, handing over the paper. 'If you need more, it will have to wait until I have secured Goyathlay, who now calls himself Geronimo.'

He seemed to take some pleasure in demonstrating that he knew the real name of his adversary. Donohue thanked him and led the girl away. She came with surprisingly good grace, and he looked at her with growing suspicion. This was not the Ysabella he had come to know and distrust.

He found out why as they climbed the pass.

She was riding in front of him where he could see her, and he had to call instructions to her as they went. She obeyed like a lamb and since lambs were new to her nature, he was on edge the whole of the way up.

'Take the track to the left!' he told her as they came to a notch in the side of the pass. It was a side trail which cut out the fort and nearly twenty miles, and would deliver them onto the pass between the Pedrogosas and the Swisshelms without having to chance the Chiricahuas to the north.

The Army might think it had the Apaches under control up there, but Donohue had been in more than one army in his life and he still considered the terms 'military' and 'intelligence' to be uneasy partners.

The girl did as she was told, and he topped out on the pass he was looking for. Night was already coming down, and he sought out a small blind side canyon with a cave in its steep wall which would keep the warmth of their fire in, and at the same time shield it from curious eyes.

He looked after the horses, and started a fire in a pocket of stones he had used before, and tucked his coffee pot into the side of the glow to heat up. Their meal was jerky and camp-fire bread, but they were both hungry enough to eat it with relish.

While they ate, she sat back against her saddle and looked him over carefully as though she had never seen him before. He shot her a glance under lowered brows and waited for her to speak. It did not take long.

'Is it that you think we have lost Luis?' she asked him.

He did not reply. He was concentrating on not looking into the fire and endangering his night vision, but mainly he was listening to the sound of the horses crunching on the thin grass around their picket pins. The mustang was as wary as any watchdog, and he knew nothing, including an Apache, would come within twenty yards of them without spooking the horse.

'If this is what you think, you are wrong,' she said. 'Luis is a fine tracker and he was raised in these mountains, above and below the border. It is how he gets on with the Apache. He knows them, and he understands them.'

Maybe, he thought. But Luis had not understood the warrior who had thrown a parting shot at him when the army caught up with Geronimo's band back in the canyons.

He nodded his thanks for the warning. If she was in the process of changing sides, he wanted her to continue it. On the other hand, she had been solidly against him in the cliff houses, and since then, only Luis's defection had happened to change her mind.

That and the opinions of the army, which had presumably been more irritating than reassuring.

He passed her a cup of coffee, and watched her sip it gingerly.

'Listen, *señorita*,' he said, and was rewarded with a flicker of the dark eyes over the rim of the cup.

'I better explain to you, so you understand what we're doin' here,' he ploughed on. He told her about finding the burning wagon and the two dead men in Sulphur Springs Valley. He explained how suspicion had been pointed at him in Tombstone, and how word had spread that he had murdered her and the men who were bringing her to Tombstone.

He described the ambush of the wagon in the canyon, and the fact that it had been carried out by men on shod horses, not Indians, and that those men had then disappeared.

'Can you think of anybody who would want you out of the way?' he asked. 'That ambush wasn't no accident. The wagon was full of simple stuff. Ranch stores, mostly, and there wasn't no secret compart-

125

ments filled with gold, nor nothin' like that.

'So what was they after, the ones who ambushed it? Was there somethin' else and I missed it?'

She gave him a surprisingly boyish grin, and shook her head.

'That wagon contained a fortune in Aztec emeralds,' she said seriously. 'I may be a simple Mexican girl, but my father, Don Pedro de Martinez, is a rich and powerful man. Hidden in that wagon was my dowry, being taken with me to meet my husband in Tombstone.'

There was a light in her eye from the firelight as she told the story which sounded a warning bell in the back of his mind. That light implied that mischief was afoot.

'That so?' he said. He did not believe a word of it, but he was delighted with her story.

'*Sí, señor,*' she said. Her expression was full of mischief. 'My father, Don Pedro, often sends his favourite daughter and a fortune in emeralds through the border country guarded only by two men who look as if they eat babies for breakfast!

'It is – how you say? – a family tradition!'

She threw her head back and laughed delightedly at his expression, and he could not resist joining in.

'How did you come to marry Barratt?'

Her expression changed like a darkening sky.

'It was my stepmother!' she said bitterly. '*Sí, señor,* there are wicked stepmothers – and my father found one specially for me!'

'What happened, then?'

'Dona Esmeralda Martinez had the one thing my

father always wanted but never had. She had old Spanish blood – pure old Spanish blood. It is impossible for any man who did not grow up in Mexican society to understand exactly what that means.

'Mexico is a land which has been divided and divided over and over again. There was originally the Indians. They warred between one another, and they bred one with another. Then came the Conquistadores. The men from Spain with their endless greed for gold and slaves. They swept away the old order in Mexico and established their own. The people who were there before – my mother's people, born there for a thousand generations – were swept away and the Spanish established their own society.'

He nodded. The impenetrable wall of aristocracy and privilege his own family had encountered in Europe and in particular in Britain was nothing new to him. He had not until now bothered to think out whether it had crossed the oceans to the new world.

He watched her, fascinated, as the bitterness came tumbling out.

'My father was born of good family, and he was a clever man. He owned land and on his land there were many things which made him rich. But one thing he could not buy, he discovered, was breeding. The breeding which would open the doors for him into the old Spanish aristocracy.'

'But if he had a beautiful wife, lovely children and plenty of money, why would he care?' asked Donohue.

Ysabella shot him a look which carried pure irritation that he did not understand life as she knew it.

'Because! Because it was the one thing he could not buy. Because it was the invisible wall he could not break down!

'While my mother lived, it was not so bad. He had a lovely home, a much loved daughter – me! – and if he ever fell into a black mood, all he had to do was look at my mother, and her beauty and her true love for him made the sun to shine once more.'

She leaned forward and refilled her cup from the coffee pot, blowing on her fingers after handling the hot metal.

'And then his wife – my mother – died. It was a bad summer that year. People – our people – drank bad water, fell ill and many died. There was an epidemic in the village and Mama would not stay at home where it was safe. She went to the village to see to the sick, and she too became sick. They could not save her, and she died.'

She drank from the coffee and pulled the collar of her coat higher on her neck. Away from the fire, it was getting bitterly cold.

'And then?' Donohue was fascinated by the tale.

'Then came Dona Maria. The Dona Maria Alvarez, of pure Castilian blood. Everything he had always wanted and could not have. Is it any wonder he was like a little boy with a big lollipop!

'But she had a reputation, that one! She was proud and she was cold – but she was also without money. She might live in a fine house, but the servants had not been paid and the furniture was slowly being sold. My father must have looked like an open gold mine to her, and she filled her hands with him and his money!'

'They married, of course?'

Her eyes flashed in the glow from the embers and her lips drew back from her teeth. He thought she looked like an angry cat.

'Of course they married! She had what he wanted and he had what she wanted and in bags full. It was not a marriage, it was a business bargain. But along with her beautiful body, came a soul shrivelled and black!'

He heard one of the horses stamp its feet suddenly, and then his mustang blew through its nose gustily. In a second he was on his feet, running to where he had picketed them. He was not quite in time to get his hand over the mustang's nose before it whinnied a challenge out into the night, a challenge that was answered from all too close for comfort.

Someone was out there, where there should be neither Indian nor white man on this cold, mountain night. And they had heard a horse challenge them.

CHAPTER SIXTEEN

Behind him there was a hiss and the faint glow of the
fire disappeared. The girl had doused it with the
coffee, which was a pity, because he had been about
to take himself an extra cup.

Out in the dark, the unknown horse whinnied
again, and his own raised its head to answer as he
clamped his hands over its nose. Was he imagining
things, or did that second whinny sound slightly
different from the first? Could there be more than
one rider out there in the dark, and if so what were
they doing travelling in the dark of such a night? It
was cold and dangerous. And whatever Crook
thought, there would be Indians about. Apaches
were not the only tribe out here, and Chiricahuas
were not the only Apaches.

And then there was Luis. But Luis was alone and
unless he had acquired some other horses, that was
not a lone rider out there.

He heard her feet coming along behind him, and
looked round to see her shadow in the gloom. She
held her own horse's head and relieved him of one

chore at least.

The moon would be up shortly, and they must move on – which would be asking for trouble since they did not know who and how many were out there – or fort up in the little cave in the side canyon. Neither alternative appealed to him.

He stood, silent and irresolute, holding the mustang's head, and used the trick of not trying to hear anything, which often led to hearing something.

In this silence, it did not. The night remained dark and soundless, though the first silvery glow over the mountains told him the moon would be up, soon.

He came to a sudden decision. He would sit tight and see what came to them. At least he would know that it could come from only one direction: the open end of the little cave.

He bent his head and told the girl what he planned in a low voice, which carried less easily at night than the sibilance of a whisper. She nodded and then said quietly, '*Sí, comprendo!*'

They led the horses back along the shallow canyon and backed them into the cave. There was a low breastwork of loose stones across half of the entrance, left there by some traveller in years gone by and he settled her down behind it, and helped her tuck herself into blankets. She hissed a request for a gun and, after hesitating for a moment, he handed her his Colt. If she planned his death, she could as easily stab him in the back as shoot him, and he reminded himself that if she had a stiletto in one boot she might just as easily have one in the other.

From the night, there came no further sound. But whoever was out there must have heard the horse whinny and had probably smelled the fire and even conceivably, the coffee and they must be sitting out there, waiting for developments, just as he was waiting in here.

'Indians? Apaches?' breathed the girl in his ear. She seemed in total control of herself, and he was reminded that she thought Luis had an arrangement with the Apache.

'Dunno,' he said. 'There's enough killers around this territory without the Apaches. There's the Pima and the Tohono O'odham, as they call themselves, and a dozen others. The army may think they got 'em under control, but the Indians don't think so, and the ones that do, occasionally have a break-out.'

He paused, remembering suddenly the shod hoof prints around the burning wagon over in the Sulphur Springs Valley.

'And then, I found the prints of shod horses near the wagon with them bodies in it. Never did work out who the hangment they might have been.'

He stopped for a second, sure he had heard movement out to the front. They lay still behind the little barricade. He was about to slip outside their refuge when the moon came up over the mountains with a rush, and the landscape turned into a pattern of black and silver.

The little side canyon looked down a spreading slope like a rock fan, and in the middle of it was a man with a rifle, caught in a frozen moment in the act of creeping up towards them.

He was as surprised by the sudden flood of silver light as they were, and for a second, froze. His face was in the shadow of his wide-brimmed sombrero, and his body made shapeless by a serape hanging over his shoulders.

As the moon shone over him he looked up and, for a long second, they were staring at his face. It was a face seen every day in Mexican communities both north and south of the border, a flat, round face with a thick, drooping moustache, teeth exposed in a moment of surprise.

'Jaime!' spat Ysabella next to him, and the Colt banged out like a howitzer. The .44 slug hit Jaime about the breastbone, and the impact knocked him flat on his back, dead before he hit the ground. His rifle clattered across the rock apron, sliding down the slope until it hit the edge of the ramp.

Instantly there were two more shots from the darkness. One hit the cliff face above them and the other presumably vanished into the darkness. Donohue did not know where it finished up.

So there had been three of them at least, and that may have been reduced to two by the girl's shot. He wondered if it had been a lucky hit, but a moment's thought convinced him it was aimed.

Silence, a silver-plated silence, fell in the canyon, and he could hear the horses shifting their hoofs restlessly.

'You knew him?' he asked her.

'I knew him! Jaime the Dog. He was like a rutting hound. No woman was safe from him – even little girls! – and he knew no shame.'

133

She spat. She sounded as though she really meant it as a cheer.

'Well, he sure knows none now. A good shot,' he muttered, turning his attention to the night. He heard her mutter agreement, and began to examine the rocks he could see outside their refuge.

One man, he decided, was among the boulders where the left-hand side of the approach ramp met the canyon wall. He saw a suggestion of movement there from time to time as though the man was having trouble settling himself, and threw a bullet into the angle, just to encourage him to keep his head down.

Instantly, a third man exposed his position by firing. He was high up, back across the main canyon behind a finger of rock reaching out from the far wall of the place, but looking straight down their throats. He proved the point by slinging a bullet down the little side canyon and into their barricade.

Splinters flew, and Donohue felt one smack into his cheek. Ysabella gave a muffled curse, but said instantly, 'I am all right. But your cheek bleeds.'

He grunted. He had more to worry about than a glancing scratch from a stone chip. In any case, he had realized he could actually see the man across the canyon when the man stood up to shoot.

The sniper had manoeuvred himself into place in the dark, and when the glare of the full moon hit the canyon, he was not as well concealed as he had thought.

Donohue extended the rifle, held it tight against

the big rock at the end of the barricade, and aimed it at the place he had last seen the man.

'*Señora,*' he said, and ignored her hiss of irritation. 'Throw another shot at the corner of the trail where the nearest of them is hiding.'

He heard her squirming into position, and then the Colt banged loudly, and as it did so, the man across the canyon popped up directly in front of his sight. He squeezed the trigger, and the Winchester thumped into his shoulder, and the target disappeared again.

There was no telling whether Donohue had scored a kill or not, and he knew he could not risk exposing them to the sniper's fire without knowing, so he squirmed round.

'See that finger of rock across the trail?' He was suddenly conscious of the warmth of her body against his own as she bent her head to follow the line of his pointing finger.

'*Sí!*'

'He's in the notch at the left of the top. Watch to see if he pops up when I fire!'

He took a bead on the corner where the nearer man had been having trouble settling himself, and squeezed off a shot. The bullet squealed away in a noisy ricochet.

'No,' said Ysabella. 'No movement, there.'

Donohue settled down to fire testing shots at the notch where man number two had concealed himself. The sharp contrast between the black shadows and the silver highlights of the canyon made shooting uncertain, and the third shot also squealed in ricochet, but it also elicited a startled shout from the target.

Donohue grinned like a wolf, and bounced another shot off the same rock. That, too squealed satisfyingly, but was accompanied with a curse and the rattle of disturbed rock.

'Enrico?' called a suddenly anxious voice. 'Enrico?'

There was no reply. Ysabella swore bitterly.

'What is the matter?' She seemed to take this very personally, but then, he had to admit to himself that being shot at in the night was a pretty personal thing.

'I know that voice!' she said. 'It is the voice of a man who works for my stepmother. A man I do not like, but a fitting companion for Jaime! Has she sent a posse after me?'

'Are you sure about the men?'

'Of course I am sure! Do you think I do not know my own household? Those two came with the Dona when she married my father. They do her . . . do you say filthy work?'

'It will do. Why are they searching for you? They ain't on no rescue mission, that's for sure.'

'They would not be. Not those animals. You say the two who my' – she could not bring herself to say the word 'husband' and contented herself with – 'that man sent to bring me here were bad men, too? They certainly did not treat me like the wife of their *jefe* while I was with them.'

'How, then?'

'They treated me like a loose woman. A woman of the streets.'

An idea was beginning to grow in him, and he did not like it one bit.

'As though it did not matter how they treated you?'

'*Sì!* And yet they must know that when I got to Tombstone I would tell the man how I had been treated. It made no sense.'

It made perfectly good sense if her husband and his chosen men knew she was not going to get to Tombstone. So did the fact that they had gone through a form of marriage when he was pretending to arrange for a big and elaborate ceremony on her arrival.

There had been no sound from either of the ambushers out in the dark, and he began to wonder if they were still there, or if he had managed to get one and the survivor had escaped.

Or – he glanced up at the opposite rim above their heads – if they had decided on a less direct approach and were even now stealing up from some unexpected direction. It would take them some time to get round on the lip of the canyon where they could shoot down into the shallow cave. But in the bright moonlight, it would not be impossible. Once a man had got up there on the opposite rim of the little canyon, he could see into the cave quite easily, and where he could see, he could shoot.

As the thought occurred to him, a little shower of sand and stones fell from the lip opposite.

CHAPTER SEVENTEEN

The first pebbles to fall into the canyon alerted Donohue and the girl, and she ducked back behind the rock rampart just as the first shot sounded.

He took off his hat and peered round the barricade at ground level. At first he could see nothing up in the rim, but after a few seconds, up where the tiny cascade of stones had started, he realized that what he though was a knob of rock had just moved, very slightly. He snatched back his head as the second shot smacked into the stone floor of the cave.

The horses, which had been increasingly restless, began to blow uneasily through their nostrils, and move around, the hoofbeats nervous and agitated. In the constricted space inside the little cave, they were becoming a menace, but Donohue and the girl could not get out of their way, and to let them out would be to lose them.

The man on the rim had to go and he had to go quickly. Donohue took a bead on the rim and waited until a slight movement up there betrayed the sniper's position.

He snatched a shot at the rim before the sniper had a chance to fire, and heard the bullet hit rock and he heard a muffled grunt. Encouraged, he sent another slug the same way without a response, and stepped out into the open canyon to get a better angle.

Instantly, there was a shot from the end of the little canyon, and a terrific blow knocked his feet out from under him, sending him thumping to the ground. His ribs hit a rock and for a second he was winded by the impact.

Surprisingly, the girl seemed to fall apart even as he fell. She screamed shrilly and burst into loud sobs and wailing. From his position on the bare rock, he could not see her properly, but he could hear her apparently throwing herself around, making the rocks in the barricade rattle, and disturbing the horses.

'No! No! Stop shooting!' she cried, shrilly. 'He is dead! You have killed him and now I have no one! Have mercy! Do not kill me!'

A gruff voice called out in Spanish from the edge of the ravine, and there was a response from the rocks at the bottom. The sniper above was telling the man at ground level whose name appeared to be Manolito, to walk up and disarm her, but Manolito was unwilling to take the chance. He had seen her kill his partner and he knew she still had the gun.

He pointed this out to his partner, who was called Diego.

'I will prove to you!' she called. The voice sounded totally unlike her usually low, musical tones. Perhaps she had panicked, he thought. Unable to see whether the man aloft could see him, he did not dare move his head to see her, and he could not call out without alerting the snipers.

'Come out where we can see you,' called the man from above. 'Prove to me you have no weapon!'

There was a short silence. Then, 'How can I prove I have nothing?'

'Think of something. It is your problem, not ours.' There was mockery in the voice, and Donohue knew what it meant.

'I would have to take off my clothes,' called the girl, and there was real fear in her voice. Donohue tried without moving to get his hands on the rifle. He had dropped it when his feet were knocked from under him, and it was lying next to him. But to get hold of the weapon, he would have to reach over his own body, and the man on the rim would see him move and shoot him without a thought.

'*Sí, señorita*, you will have to take off your clothes!' The voice from the rim sounded as if it were licking its lips. 'The choice is yours. There is no other help for you.'

She hesitated for another long moment, then, 'I will do it!' It was almost a sob, and the man at the bottom of the canyon sniggered, and stood up. He jumped down from his pile of rocks, and started up the canyon.

At the same time, the man on the rim stood up, and holding his rifle in one hand, started to climb down the rim towards the notch which had sheltered his friend. His head was turned back to watch when the girl emerged into the moonlight, and she did so just as he reached the end of the low cliff and turned to climb down.

Even in the moment of highest danger, Donohue found time to be stunned at the sight of her.

In the moonlight, she was a silver and black statue of incredible beauty, walking out onto the canyon floor. One arm was protectively across her breasts and the other hand held downwards to preserve her modesty. She was shuffling rather than walking and her hair had fallen forward over her eyes.

'*Hola*! *Guapa*!' sniggered Manolo from down the canyon, who was enjoying himself hugely. 'You know what will happen now?' He held his hands apart, rifle held by the barrel in his right, and Donohue noticed he also wore his handgun on the right.

The other man was making his way down from the lip. Distracted by the naked girl, he missed his footing, and was forced to drop his rifle to grab a hold. At the same time, he turned his head away.

Like a striking snake she brought her hand out from between her thighs. The hand held across her breasts also, it turned out, cradled his Colt, and she shot Manolo through his stomach at only a few yards' range.

Donohue rolled over and pulled the rifle into his shoulder as he did so. The climbing Diego was trying to hang onto the rock and get his pistol out at the same time, but he already knew that he was too late. Donohue's bullet entered his chest below his armpit and smashed through his chest, destroying his heart and shredding both lungs as it went. He was dead before he even started to fall.

When he looked back, the girl was standing over Manolo and all semblance of modesty was gone. She stood, one hand on her naked hip and the other pointing the Colt at his head.

Manolo was in shock and the agony of his wound had not yet started to bite through. The bullet had broken his back and he was able only to move his upper body and arms, but he lay still with his eyes filled with the muzzle of the big pistol.

'You were going to tell me what you would do to me, Manolito,' the girl said in her normal, mellow voice. 'Well, go on, tell me!'

The man shifted his attention from the gun and stared into her eyes.

'It is of no matter, now, *señorita*,' he said. 'I know that my back is broken, for I cannot move my legs. All that will come to me now is pain and, a long time later, death. Too long! Kill me, now!'

She shrugged. 'Why?'

'I do not want to live through the pain, that is why!'

'And what did you have planned for me, Manolito? A lifetime of luxury and joy? A loving home and a dozen children?

'Na, Mano! My future would have been short and nasty and painful, and you would have enjoyed every second of it! Ask no mercy of me, *cerdo*! You shall

142

receive from me what you would have given.'

'*Por favour, señorita*! Have compassion! Have mercy!'

She started to turn away, then as suddenly swung back.

'There is one thing you can do for me,' she said, and the man's face slackened in surprise. 'You can tell me what your orders were.'

He shrugged expressively.

'The Dona Maria sent us to kill, *señorita*. Just to kill. She wants to make sure she is the only one to benefit from the will of your father, I think.'

'But my father is not dead.'

The man's eyes slid away and he gave a small shrug.

'It pains me greatly, *señorita*, to tell you that your father passed away the morning after you left the rancho to travel to your bridegroom.'

She gave a short bark of laughter, though it turned into a sob.

'How did he die?'

'He was taken ill after his breakfast, *señorita*. The sickness progressed very quickly which is not surprising because it involved the venom of the rattlesnake. A doctor was called, but alas, he was an old man and frail. He was dead before noon.

'It pains me to tell you this, and in such circumstances, but you are the sole survivor of your father's line – and the Dona Maria is very concerned that she should be the sole survivor.'

'Who killed him?'

The words were ground out. The dying man gave

a bitter, sideways smile.

'The Dona Maria is a very determined woman, *señorita*. She would entrust this important task to nobody else. She administered the venom, and she sent us to make sure there would be no loose ends to the story.'

He gave a sudden spasm and cried out in a harsh voice.

'We missed you in the Sulphur Springs Valley. Then again at the fort, where Luis took you. We thought we had you in the ruins where he was trying to sell you to Geronimo as a slave, but your new friend came and took you from there. And now. . . .'

Suddenly his right hand whipped out from beneath his serape, holding a pistol.

A shot slammed out, deafening in the narrow defile, but Manolo's pistol was already falling from his hand.

'Never let 'em chatter, *señora*,' said Donohue, levering another cartridge into the rifle. 'Always gives 'em the drop. They know when they are goin' to act, and you can only react. Only safe sidewinder's a sidewinder with its head blowed off!'

She let the pistol hang down by her side, and fell against him, shivering with cold and shock. He put his arm round her, acutely conscious of her nakedness, and was about to make suitable soothing noises when he felt her stiffen and pull away from him.

'*Cerdo!*' she spat. 'All men are the same! You take advantage of a naked woman. You try to maul her.

Pig!' she added, in case he had not got the message in Spanish, and for emphasis, she slapped his face.

It was no lover's tap. Donohue, caught totally by surprise, did not even have a chance to duck, and took the full force of the blow on his cheekbone. It hurt.

'I never intended. . . .' He began. 'I had forgotten you had no clothes on, ma'am! Didn't mean to . . .' He stopped, dumbfounded, when she slapped him again.

'That is for forgetting! And that—' Her hand swung again, but this time, he caught her wrist and stopped it.

'And what the hangment is that one for?' he shouted, goaded beyond bearing.

'That is for not intending to!' she snapped, stepped round him and dived into the little cave. He stood there by three corpses and waited for his head to stop ringing. When it had, he could still not work out whether he had just been slapped for taking advantage of her nudity, or for not doing so.

Whatever the reason, he still felt the best thing they could do was to get away from the scene as fast as they could. Even the sleepiest Indian hearing repeated shots in the night, would be tempted to come and see what they concerned.

And then there was Luis. Had she missed the implications of Manolo's dying words, or taken them to heart? He suspected the second, but it was possible that this wilful, surprising woman had simply refused to believe them because they came from a man she despised.

One way or another, he told himself, he needed to take her to Tombstone, and to Tombstone she would go, come hell, high-water or the Butterfield Stage!

CHAPTER EIGHTEEN

And so to Tombstone they went.

The trail was cold, and a wicked wind scoured the land, making them huddle into their coats, and tie down their hats. Donohue knotted his bandanna over her nose and mouth and sunk his chin into his collar to try and keep the blowing dust out of his teeth.

The horses were skittish when they set out, uncomfortable at being trapped in the little cave during the gunfight, but a period plodding through the wind calmed them down, and they put their heads down and walked forward stubbornly.

Donohue stopped to rest them and give them a drink every couple of hours, and they covered the ground well enough.

Ysabella took to the trail like a veteran. She rode behind him when the trail was narrow and alongside him when there was space enough. Every time they stopped, she made a fire and boiled water for coffee, and managed to gather up enough twigs and kindling for the next stop.

147

'Have we much further?' she asked at one stop. They were camped in the lee of a knoll, and the horses had found some sparse grass and were cropping busily.

Donohue sipped his coffee and wrapped his gloved hand round the cup. The liquid was black as night and strong enough to revive the dead, exactly what they needed.

'About another couple of hours,' he said. 'It will be dark when we get in, which ain't no bad thing. With luck we can get to the deputy before any hothead recognizes me and takes a shot.'

'We must look out for Luis, then,' she said. She was chewing on a strip of jerky and her voice was indistinct.

'You reckon he's following you?'

'No. You!' she said. 'I have known Luis for long, but one thing I do know, he will be very angry you took me away from him. He is out there, somewhere, and he will not be put off!'

He was puzzled. 'Seemed to me you were good friends with him, up there in the ruins. Not so?'

'Friends? Not exactly. I have known Luis for years. He is . . . He was the bad boy every girl thinks she needs in her life. My father did not like him at all, and warned me against him many times, but I did not listen.

'When I left the wagon, I hid. The men looked for me, but they could not find me – but Luis found me immediately.'

'Almost as though he had been trailing you and saw you escape?'

'Exactly as though he had been watching, *si*! He had been tracking us and waiting his chance. He had promised to get me back to my father, but already I was wondering why he was taking me back to Bowie when we should have been moving south.'

Donohue sucked a tooth and watched her carefully.

'He was going to hand me over to the Apaches to hide me, or so he said. But Apaches and Mexicans are not kind to one another. There is too much . . . too much history between us. I think he was selling me to them, and that was why he could speak with the warriors. They wanted me!'

'. . . and shot at him when they saw they were not going to get you,' said Donohue. A man who would sell a Mexican woman alive to the Apaches was beyond understanding. The Apaches saved their most fiendish cruelties for women, and for Mexican women in particular.

The girl stared at him over the fire and nodded.

'He said he would take me back to my father. But now I think my father must have been dead by then. Luis was sent, I think, to kill me. That woman was not putting her trust in just one gang, she was covering her bets with another.'

'But why does she hate you so much? Out of the country and married to an American you would be just as far out of her way as in the grave.'

She shook her head with a quirky smile.

'People do not come back from the grave to seek you out, *amigo*! She knew I might easily come back from Tombstone. And there was the money.'

'What money?'

She laughed, delightedly.

'Suddenly, I have all your attention! The money she thinks she will inherit when my father and I are dead.'

'She only thinks?'

'*Sí!* She thinks that my father had a hoard of emeralds, and that his fortune is based on that.'

'And he did not have?'

She shot the dregs of her coffee over the ashes of the fire.

'Sadly not, *amigo.* His fortune was all based on his contracts to supply the army of my country. When he died, so did the contracts. Oh, there will be some money left. If she is careful, it will last her for a few years. But not the fortune she thought she was marrying.

'She had her *bandidos* murder the provider of her riches. I will mourn my Papa. . . .' The word caught in her throat, and suddenly she was rocking backwards and forwards, sobbing bitterly.

Donohue was genuinely embarrassed. He had no experience in handling sobbing women. Western women, ranchers' wives, farmers' drudges, saloon women, were not given to tears, however much they might feel like it at times. They set their teeth, rolled up their sleeves, harnessed a team or loaded their muskets, and simply learned to cope.

He wrapped one arm round her heaving shoulders and patted her gently, making the kind of noises he would use to calm a hurt animal.

And suddenly her arms were round his neck and

her tearful eyes were looking into his.

'Well, fool,' she said, 'are you going to kiss me or not?'

It was after dark when they rode into Tombstone, and tied the horses up at the hitching rail outside the office at the courthouse.

Tombstone was going full blast. The rattle of pianos came from the honky tonks and the voices were loud and the laughter shrill.

Normal enough – and yet Donohue thought he could detect a different quality in the din, an almost hysterical note in the laughter and a feverish rhythm in the music. He helped Ysabella down from her tired horse, and left the animals to drink from a water trough.

There was a light inside the little lock-up and when he pounded on the door, he heard boots crossing the floor before the upper half of the thick door opened and Art Knowles looked out.

He was standing back, at the hinge side of the door and by shifting his head slightly, Donohue could see the deputy had a shotgun in his hand pointing through the gap and straight at Donohue's stomach.

'Now, you be right careful where you point that thing, Deputy!' he said warily. 'I got my witness here, and I don't want the law blowin' her away and makin' me a liar.'

There was a snort from Ysabella next to him, but she stepped nimbly enough away from Knowles's line of fire. The deputy let down the hammer from full

cock and pointed the gun at the floor, his face breaking into a grin in the yellow light of the lamp.

'You found the girl and she's alive?' he said
delightedly. 'Glory be! I'da put money on it myself,
but Johnny Behan swore she had to be dead!'

He led them into the room, where Wyatt Earp was
sitting in outdoor clothes, cleaning a Colt which had
an enormously long barrel. He glanced up and
nodded at Donohue gravely. He seemed on edge and
serious.

'See here, Wyatt! Donohue found the girl!'
Knowles was as excited as though he had brought her
in himself. The lawman slipped the cylinder back
into the frame of the gun and ran the spindle down
through it before spinning the empty cylinder and
opening the loading gate.

'Glad you're alive and well, *señorita*!' he said
soberly and stared long and hard at her. While he
looked, she pulled off her outer wrappings, and even
Donohue was surprised at the transformation. She
turned from a picture of a shabby saddle tramp into
the striking woman he knew her to be, simply by
peeling off layers.

'Thank you *Señor* Earp,' she said, dignified as a
dowager. 'It has been a long ride to get here, and the
journey has been perilous.'

Donohue blinked at her poise but remembered
her father had sent her to Europe to finish her
education, and that money had not been spared on
it. The wildcat killer who had stripped to her skin to
put the hired assassins off their stroke long enough
to kill them had another side to her. No less danger-

ous, but surprisingly polished.

Earp nodded at her and slipped shells into the long barrelled pistol, then dropped it in turn into his holster.

Knowles said, 'Nobody waitin' across the street, Wyatt.'

Donohue looked at him, surprised. When he had last been here, there had been tension in the air, but the Earps had seemed to ride it easily enough.

'What's wrong?' he asked.

'There was a showdown with The Cowboys a couple of days back,' said Knowles. 'Wyatt, Morgan and Virgil and Doc Holliday shot it out with them outside Fly's photographic studio back of the OK Corral. Tom and Frank McLaury and Billy Clanton was killed. Town's divided over whether it was legal and who started it.'

Donohue understood the tension in town. With three men from one side dead, and the town unable to make up its mind who was in the right, no wonder nerves were on edge. But since the Earps were lawmen, he fully expected the law to be behind them.

'Some gun battle, huh?' he ventured.

'Didn't last two minutes,' the deputy told him. 'Bound to come to it, I guess, but it's left the town divided. The survivors on The Cowboys' side swear they tried to avoid a fight, say the Earps forced it on 'em!'

Donohue kept his mouth shut. He knew the Earps had seemed determined on a showdown, but from what he had heard, The Cowboys had been just as aggressive about it. And the Earps were the appointed marshals in the area.

Whatever the outcome, it was none of his business, and he devoted himself to registering Ysabella's existence with the law.

Whatever the risks, it was necessary for the citizens of Tombstone to see her, alive, in their town. There were, as he had already seen, far too many trigger happy citizens eager to shoot first and ask questions afterward.

Knowles fussed like a dog with puppies on their way through the town. Barratt was reported to be playing cards in the back of the Occidental, which was doing less than its usual roaring trade. The town seemed to be on edge since the OK Corral shooting, and prudent citizens stayed away from the bigger saloons, which tended to identify with one side or the other. Nobody wanted to be an innocent party in a shoot-out, and Tombstone knew in its bones that this affair had not ended with the deaths of the McLaurys and Billy Clanton.

Barratt was sitting at the far end of the saloon when they shouldered their way through the batwings. The room was half empty and most of the men were drinking at the bar or playing cards. There were a couple of saloon girls trying to work up some trade, and a man with his shirt-sleeves held up with two women's garters was rattling at the piano keys. The effect was more depressing than comforting.

Barratt was just making a bet when Donohue led

Ysabella across the floor to his table. He did not immediately recognize either of them, muffled up as they were in their coats.

He glanced up from his cards and saw merely two muffled men standing at the opposite side of the table.

'If you're after work, go to the freight office in the morning, and Branson will tell you if there's anything going,' he said. 'With this weather there isn't a lot moving, but I could do with some drivers.'

'Ain't that, Mr Barratt,' Donohue told him, in a voice calculated to travel round the bar. 'We brought you a present that's been worryin' you for a time!'

Barratt looked at him hard for the first time, and his eyes widened as he recognized Donohue at last.

'You!' he said, putting down his cards on the table. 'I thought you got more sense than to come back into town after what you done!'

Donohue unbuttoned his coat and loosened his scarf. Reaching down, he pushed the coat back from his gun, and rested his right hand on it. The three men in the card school hastily started to stand up.

'Set tight, boys,' Donohue told them, easily. 'This won't take but a moment.'

He stabbed his finger at Barratt, deliberately taking it away from his gun.

'I'll just take a moment of your time, folks. There's been a lot o' loose talk round town that I held up one of Mr Barratt's wagons, murdered two of his employees, and treated his fiancée real bad, then murdered her and hid her body!'

Barratt was beginning to regain his balance.

'Nothing loose about that talk, Donohue. That's exactly what you did. How else did you come by my poor fiancée's traps? Nobody else could have done it. You robbed and murdered her, despite all two of my best men could do, then you tried to burn the evidence!'

'So you have proof your fiancée's dead?'

Barratt must have been as aware of the silence in the room as anybody else. He was not a popular man in Tombstone, but he had, at least until now, had the town's sympathy. Now, it did not seem quite so clear-cut. What was the alleged murderer doing back in town, for one thing? Surely a real killer of two men and one woman would have made good his escape by now?

'It breaks my heart to say so in front of all these good citizens, but I know she is dead.' he said loudly. 'And I have proof that you are the murderer. You made a big mistake coming back here, Donohue! Tombstone does not have any time for rapists and the murderers of women!'

There was still no sound of popular support from the bar. The men were listening intently, and the bar girls' faces were set masks.

'Knowles, you are a deputy sheriff and an officer of the law,' said Barratt. 'I call upon you to take this man under arrest for the murder of Ysabella Martinez, my dear fiancée!'

As he said it, his eye fell on Ysabella, who had been standing half behind Donohue. While the two men had been talking, she had been unwinding the scarf from her neck and unbuttoning her coat.

156

Now, as she started to take off her hat and shake out her mane of black hair, Barratt realized who she was. His face froze and for a moment he was unable to speak.

'But Ysabella Martinez is not dead, as you see, *Señor* Barratt!' she said. 'She lives, despite everything you have tried to do to bring about her end! She lives, thanks to the devotion and courage of the very man you falsely accuse of murder and rape!'

Barratt got his voice back to croak, 'This woman is not Ysabella Martinez! The killer has brought an impostor to clear himself of suspicion! This is some bar girl he has hired to. . . .'

Donohue's nerves, which had been stretched to breaking point for days of fighting and riding through some of the toughest and most dangerous country on earth, snapped and took his temper along with it.

He took a long step forward, grabbed Barratt by the collar of his black broadcloth coat, and dragged him across the table, scattering chips and cards as he came.

'You call this fine young woman a bar girl?' he roared. 'This woman has been betrayed by you, by her family, by a man who called himself her friend!

'She has ridden nigh a hundred miles in the worst weather of the year, fought Indians, Mexican bandits and the coyotes you sent to Mexico to bring her back here to her death!'

Barratt struggled furiously with the big, hard hand which had him by the throat.

Donohue pulled him off the table and let go and

Barratt, caught off balance, tripped and fell to his knees. He was livid with rage, and the intensity of his anger betrayed him.

He grabbed for his hip, and came to his feet at the same moment, a gun in his hand. The men at the bar hit the floor in a long practised reaction to gunplay in the town's saloons.

Donohue shot him cleanly between the eyes.

The report of the gun seemed unnaturally loud in the room, and it was followed by an equally unnatural silence.

Barratt's hand became lifeless and the gun dropped from it to the floor with a clatter. Then the dead man's knees folded, and he fell to the floor like a pile of wet washing.

For a man who aspired to be an important figure in the newly born town of Tombstone, it was a surprisingly undramatic death. One moment he was a living hating human being, drawing his concealed gun, and the next he was a pile of clothes on a splintered pine board floor.

The collectively held breath of the bar-room crowd was released in a collective 'whoosh'. One man spoke the thoughts of them all.

'Man, that was *shootin'*!' said Art Knowles. 'That surely was *shootin'*!'

The barman, who knew a buying crowd when he saw one, shouted, 'Gennelmen, we have been watchin' a legend bein' born! First drink free for them as wants to be part of history!'

It turned out to be a record night for a bar which became history in itself, but Donohue and Ysabella were no longer there to join in when that free first drink had been served. The customers cheerfully bought the second drink and all subsequent drinks themselves, and within two more rounds, they had forgotten all about the tired couple in mud-spattered clothes who had come, killed and disappeared again.

Several men later swore they had seen the mysterious pair in towns as far apart as Santa Fe and Prescott, doing anything from running saloons to appearing on stage, but they were all wrong.

They were too busy raising a family on their ranch in the Superstitions to do any of those things.

FOOTNOTE

'But, grandma,' protested her fourth grandchild, sitting on the stoop one night as the Arizona sunset bathed them all in a red glow, and the rattle of pans from the kitchen told the enthralled children that they had been listening to Grandma's tall tales for quite long enough.

'But, Grandma, what happened to Luis?'

He grandmother flicked a look over the child's head to her husband who was carefully cleaning out his pipe.

'Oh, he just disappeared, and we never heard from him again, *querida*. Now go and wash your hands for supper, there's a good girl.'

Donohue noisily blew through the empty pipe and tapped it for the last time on his heel. He knew what had happened to Luis. But he was not telling his wife. There had always been a slightly misty look in her eye when the man's name came up, and Luis had, after all, been the romantically wicked lover every woman should have in her past.

The emphasis, in the case of Luis, was on the 'past'. And in the past he would safely stay.

OUR FRIEND THE DOG SERIES

Edited by ROWLAND JOHNS

OUR FRIEND THE
WEST HIGHLAND

OUR FRIEND THE DOG SERIES

Edited by
ROWLAND JOHNS

*Simply written, wise guidance for those who keep,
or intend to keep, dogs, bitches, or puppies of every
popular breed.*

A TYPICAL WEST HIGHLAND WHITE TERRIER

Our Friend
THE WEST HIGHLAND
WHITE TERRIER

Edited by
ROWLAND JOHNS

WITH A FRONTISPIECE

METHUEN & CO. LTD.
36 ESSEX STREET W.C.
London

First published, April 25th 1935
Second Edition, January 1947
Third Edition October 1950
Fourth Edition, 1954
Reprinted 1959

4.2

CATALOGUE NO. 4221/U

PRINTED AND BOUND IN GREAT BRITAIN BY
BUTLER AND TANNER LTD., FROME AND LONDON

CONTENTS

*The frontispiece is of Rowberrow Roland (by Dick Turpin of
Dane End—Rowberrow Runnaduck) and is reproduced by kind permission of his owner, Mrs. Thornton, Rowberrow Kennels, Wood-
pecker Farm, Warren Row, Wargrave, Berks.*

OUR FRIEND THE WEST HIGHLAND

CHAPTER I

THE ORIGIN OF THE BREED

PROBABLY as much controversy has raged over the beginnings of the West Highland Terrier as over any breed of dog. Some authorities have stated definitely that the breed is simply a white variant of the Scottish Terrier and not a distinct breed at all. The romanticists, on the other hand, link them up with some 'Spanish White Dogs' that are said to have been landed on the Island of Skye when ships of the Spanish Armada came to grief on that wild coast. Others hold that the breed was evolved by the late Colonel E. D. Malcolm of Poltalloch, although Colonel Malcolm himself never made such a claim. It is clear that in earlier times what is now known as the West Highland White was generally called the Poltalloch Terrier; but for the beginnings of the breed we should have to go back much farther. Sir Ian Malcolm informed the writer that the breed were kept and highly esteemed at Poltalloch, the family's Argyllshire seat, over 100 years ago, but even then they were no newfangled creation. In the sixteenth century there were in Argyllshire 'earth dogges' of sufficient repute to justify frequent complimentary references in print by contemporary chroniclers of the chase; and those were the days when a man or a dog had to be something out of the ordinary to find his way into a book. These dogs took the eye of King James the Sixth of Scotland and First of England, and when he had the fancy to send a present of dogs to a friend in France it was the 'earth dogges or terrieres' out of Argyllshire that were his choice. Some of these gift dogs may have been white in colour, but probably they were not, for in olden times there was a prejudice against white dogs. The impression seems to have been widespread that they lacked strength and stamina, and white puppies were accordingly destroyed by the breeders. However, either because some breeders were more sensible than others, or because specimens persisted in cropping up even in families where the colour-bar was rigorously imposed, white strains survived to give the lie eventually to the suggestion that they were lacking in any of the attributes of the ideal terrier. Hence, over a century ago they were bred and used, not only at Poltalloch but throughout Argyllshire, and quite a number were kept and esteemed in Ross-shire and the Isle of Skye. Probably few of them were pure white, for in pre-show days there was no insistence upon immaculacy of colour. Over sixty years ago a visitor to the Poltalloch kennels described the dogs as being ' a sort of linty white in colour '. Even to this day in Argyllshire a touch of pale red or yellow is not accounted a fault, as a hide-bound show standard is not of much account in purely sporting strains. Apart, however, from the question of colour (pure white being *de rigueur* in dogs with show pretensions) the description of the West Highland White (or rather Poltalloch) Terrier of those early days approximates very nearly in its main essentials to the official standard obtaining to-day, which is given elsewhere in this book. The main difference is in weight, the present maximum of eighteen pounds being two pounds less than was acceptable in late Victorian times.

As to the suggestion that the breed were merely white-coloured Scotties, Colonel Malcolm more than once stated most emphatically that this was not so, and that any idea of judging them on Scottish Terrier lines would be entirely wrong. And as for the idea that the West Highland White lacks some of the attributes of the ideal sporting terrier, Robert Leighton, in his *Complete Book of the Dog*, records an incident in which a young dog, bred by Colonel Malcolm and given to a keeper, was concerned. It had been practically disembowelled by its fierce adversary in a fox-cairn, and came back to its master for help. The keeper was rendering first aid when the dog slipped out of his hands, re-entered the cairn and forced the fox into the open. There are many well-authenticated stories of the same kind concerning the West Highland

White Terrier, and it is small wonder that a student and admirer of the breed once said, ' No water was ever too cold, and no earth was ever too deep for them.'

CHAPTER II

THE CHARACTER OF THE BREED

IT may be said of a number of terrier breeds (which shall here be nameless) that apart from their external characteristics they are 'much of a muchness'. In saying this there is no intention of belittling their many splendid qualities. But the West Highland White Terrier's virtues and traits single him out from the rest. He is an individualist, a 'character' as distinct from his contemporaries in terrier-dom as it is possible for a terrier to be. Of his tenacity and never-say-die spirit an inkling has already been given ; but that is only one of the many admirable facets to his character. As to externals, none can deny the charm, friendliness, strength and activity that a glance at the breed conveys. The self-esteem ·that the standard stipulates shall be a part of his equipment reveals itself to his friends not in the form of an aggressive

cocksureness, but rather as a jaunty, genial
confidence in himself. In the domestic circle
he is a jolly companion who fits unobtrusively
into the scheme of things. He shows a good-
natured tolerance towards visitors of the desirable kind, although many of the other sort
have had good reason to regret that the teeth
of a West Highland are unusually large for the
size of the dog. As a puppy he is one of the
easiest of all breeds to house-train, and even
when taken from outdoor kennels his acquisi-
tion of the civilized manners of a well-ordered
household is a mere matter of days. Another
not unimportant virtue of especial interest to
those who travel a good deal and like to take
their dogs with them : they are extraordinarily
keen on motoring. At a certain well-known
kennels there is great competition among the
doggy denizens for places in the car when a
run is contemplated—and great disappointment among those left behind. And they are
especially well behaved when staying in hotels
and give far less trouble in strange surroundings than most breeds. If all dogs were like
the West Highland the present reluctance of
many *hôteliers* to accommodate canine guests

would soon disappear. Even in puppyhood his behaviour in the house leaves little room for criticism, for although he has his full share of high spirits it is extremely seldom that he goes berserk and attacks the carpets and curtains. The breed is blessed with an extraordinarily retentive memory, and a breeder assured the writer that dogs she had bred and parted from in puppyhood always remembered her if she met them as grown dogs. She had met some of her former puppies after an interval of two years and these had shown unmistakable signs of recognition as soon as they saw her. They have about them, too, something of that mysteriousness found in most Highlanders. That meaning 'sixth sense' or second sight often displays itself. A well-known breeder once had a dog who, when she happened to be away from home, always knew when her return was imminent no matter for how long she had been absent. And the strange thing is that these 'manifestations' always happened exactly ten minutes before the lady reached the house, despite the fact that the car in which she was travelling must then have been four or five miles away.

The dog's behaviour can hardly be explained by acuteness of hearing for there must often have been many other cars nearer to the house. Another dog when left at home was always able to tell whether her absence would be long or short, although the preparations for departure were never made in his presence. If she was just going out for a few hours he would go upstairs and curl up on the foot of her bed to await her return. But if the absence was for a week-end or longer he always knew that it was no use returning to the bedroom, and accordingly stayed downstairs.

The members of the breed are very good-tempered and tolerant towards one another. It cannot be said of every breed that one can turn out a whole lot of dogs together in a run in the practical certainty that peace and harmony will reign. It is a pleasant sight to see a dozen or so West Highlands of all ages romping together in an enclosure in the greatest good-fellowship.

Like all the terrier tribe the West Highland dearly loves a rat-hunt and needs little or no encouragement in this where there are opportunities. Unfortunately they are rather notori-

ous as poachers and have sometimes been
known to lead gun-dogs permanently from
the paths of virtue. So it behoves owners in
districts where game is plentiful and keepers
are not too sympathetic to keep a watchful
eye for any signs of the marauding instinct.
The breed's sporting proclivities have another
disadvantage, particularly in their native Scotland. When used to bolt foxes the most ven-
turesome and plucky dogs sometimes squeeze
their way into inaccessible crevices in the
rocks from which they cannot escape or be
released, and are often lost for good.

The breed seems to grow old more grace-
fully than many, and those big strong teeth
are usually retained in good condition longer
than is usual with other breeds. And deaf-
ness, that bane of certain other breeds whose
coats are white, is hardly ever met with except
in old dogs whose faculties generally are on the
wane. The West Highland, if properly cared
for, lives happily and healthily to a good old
age. It is not unusual to find them still in
splendid form at eleven or twelve years.

The West Highland White Terrier has always
had a steadfast following. His popularity owes

nothing to 'boosting' by interested parties, and as a consequence he is not subject to those meteoric rises and severe slumps that affect breeds whose supporters allow enthusiasm to outrun discretion. Proof of the secure position which the breed holds in the affections of its admirers is afforded by Kennel Club statistics, which show that over a period of ten years the registrations of the West Highland White Terrier have fluctuated less than those of any other popular breed. The breed's supporters have never gone in for mass-production methods, and the demand for good West Highland puppies is such that there are not enough to go round.

CHAPTER III

BUYING A WEST HIGHLAND

B UYING a dog, and especially a puppy, is a highly speculative transaction, but the risks can be greatly minimized if careful forethought is given. The first question the intending buyer should bear in mind is the purpose for which the dog is required. If a domestic pet is sought the sex question arises. The impression is very widespread that a bitch calls for endless vigilance, but this is an unjustifiable slur on the sex. Apart from a spell of two or three weeks occurring twice a year bitches are less troublesome than dogs. They are more faithful and affectionate ; they are, if anything, more conscientious in their duties as domestic guards ; and they are more amenable to discipline, although they do not lag behind their brethren when a sporting or ratting expedition is afoot. In addition, owing to the undue stress placed upon their draw-

12

backs, they are cheaper—and this is a consideration in these days of economy.

If the dog is required purely as a house-dog, quality is not so paramount as when the purchaser has breeding or show ambitions. A young puppy of a good but not outstanding strain can be had for a fairly reasonable sum. It is always a good thing for the novice buyer to consult some one who has a good knowledge of the points of the breed and if possible to secure the approval of this person before finally concluding the transaction.   Apart from the question whether the puppy is a good specimen of the breed there is also the question of physical condition.   Such things as unsound teeth, ear troubles, rickets or skin trouble are to be avoided and defects of this kind are not always patent to the novice.   Failing the co-operation of a knowledgeable but disinterested fancier, it is well worth while to make the purchase subject to the inspection and approval of a veterinary surgeon, who for a reasonable fee will examine and report on a puppy's condition.   The expenditure of a guinea or so in this manner may save endless expense for veterinary treatment later on.   An additional

safeguard worthy of adoption is to make a
point of dealing only with members of one of
the big specialist clubs, such as the West Highland White Terrier Club of England. These
people have a reputation to maintain and pur-
chasers may rely upon getting a square deal
from them. When one is dealing with an
unknown stranger living at a distance it is
best to utilize one of the ' deposit and approval '
schemes conducted by the doggy newspapers.
For a small charge both breeder and purchaser
are safeguarded and the money is not handed
over until the purchaser has notified his satisfaction with his bargain. Any dealer who
objects to conducting the transaction on these
lines should be avoided.

When breeding is the objective it is better
to seek a mature brood bitch of proven capacity
rather than a puppy or a maiden bitch, as
the risk of barrenness is thus avoided. In the
selection of a brood bitch to form the founda-
tion of a kennel the utmost care should be
employed. Although in making one's choice
the official standard of show points should not
be lost sight of, it should be borne in mind
that the bitch's main purpose in life is to

produce good puppies. But although the bitch of one's choice may fall far short of show perfection, weediness should be avoided, as also should any flagrant faults. Other matters affecting the choice of a brood bitch are dealt with in the chapter on breeding.

As for buying a West Highland with the main intention of using him for sporting purposes, almost any well-bred specimen will, when put to the test, be a credit to the breed when he goes to ground. Dogs that have come of a long line of followers of the chase will, however, be likely to outshine dogs of a show strain in this particular sphere, though their external make-up would not take a show judge's eye. But beware of some of the specious advertisements that sometimes appear, purporting to offer perfect paragons at knock-down prices, and if the flowery language employed tempts you to chance your luck, always bear in mind, and use, the safeguards mentioned earlier on in this chapter.

CHAPTER IV

ADVICE TO NOVICE BREEDERS

THERE are two pieces of advice to the novice breeder that it is safe to say would always be given by successful breeders who have already been 'through the mill'. The first is to begin with a brood bitch who is a proven matron, and the second is to buy the very best bitch that one's purse will allow. It is always unwise to economize in a matter of this kind, when the expenditure of a few extra pounds may make all the difference between success and failure, and in any event will have a far-reaching effect upon the fortunes of one's kennel. The writer has on more than one occasion heard the suggestion that as a beginning a novice should purchase two brood bitches, the idea being that success is more likely if one takes more than one chance in the breeding lottery. The idea, however, is a thoroughly unsound one, for the novice is much more liable to err than the experienced breeder, and he should reduce the chances of error to a minimum.

As mentioned in a previous chapter, the brood bitch, although she may not be of a type that would win distinction on the show bench, should be free from any but venial faults, for it is a mistake to suppose that any serious shortcomings can be compensated for by a corresponding excellence in the stud-dog. The most likely type of bitch to buy is one that has already produced a litter that has been shown with success in puppy classes. Before the deal is finally clinched examination by a veterinary surgeon is strongly advised, so that one may be assured of the bitch's soundness.

The choice of a brood bitch having been made, and the approximate date of coming into season having been ascertained, steps should be taken to requisition the services of a suitable stud-dog. This is a matter which should be arranged well in advance, for as stud-dogs of repute are in considerable demand and are only allowed to undertake a limited number of services, delay may mean that the chosen dog is not available, and that one must rest content with the services of the second-best dog, who may not be nearly as suitable.

It is a good plan for the novice to acquaint himself beforehand with something of the theory of breeding. Mendelism, that theory of inheritance which now finds wide acceptance, will well repay study, as a knowledge of its laws regarding the transmission of characteristics from parents to offspring may prove of great value. There are a number of excellent handbooks on the subject, such as *Mendelism and Evolution*, by E. B. Ford, which the earnest novice is recommended to read. There is no infallible recipe for the production of first-class stock, but neither is it a proceeding in which rule-of-thumb methods are likely to produce satisfactory results. The most successful breeders are those who have made a serious study of the subject's many problems.

To the novice breeder membership of a specialist club may prove invaluable—especially at the onset when important decisions have to be taken. In the choice of a stud-dog, for example, the advice of experienced breeders with an extensive knowledge of blood-lines may be worth a great deal, and the surest way of getting into touch with such helpful people is by joining a specialist club.

The stud-dog's services having been arranged for and the bitch carefully conditioned by regular exercise and suitable feeding so that she carries no excess of fat, it remains to await the arrival of the œstrum. Its imminent approach will be marked by restlessness in the bitch and a desire for the company of other dogs. This phase is succeeded by a local inflammation and a discharge, light in colour, which becomes progressively darker. The best time for mating is from the ninth to the eleventh day after the beginning of the discharge, and it is wise to arrange for the arrival at the stud-dog's quarters a day or two in advance of that time in order that the bitch may become used to her surroundings and overcome any slight antipathy that she may show towards the stud-dog. Sometimes in order to 'make sure' a second service is given two days after the first, but this cannot be taken for granted unless it has been previously arranged for. It is always best to have the details of arrangements for service clearly set down in writing, as memories are sometimes short, and verbal promises often give rise to dispute over their precise terms. When the stud-dog's kennels are a long distance away and it is necessary to send the bitch by train one of the special travelling-boxes or baskets should be used. Those with a sloping roof are best as they are less liable to have other articles placed upon them when in transit with consequent impairment of ventilation. The sending of brood bitches by rail should be avoided at week-ends as delays often occur. Where the journey is a very long one, possibly involving changes, a request to give water *en route* should be affixed to the travelling-box. The stud-dog's owner should be notified by telephone or telegram of the time the bitch is due to arrive, and should also be acquainted beforehand of the bitch's preferences as regards diet.

Upon her return home after mating the bitch's normal routine should be resumed, and unless her appetite shows signs of failing there need be no departure from her customary diet. Three or four weeks after mating, however, the quantity and variety of food can be increased. Fish can sometimes be given instead of meat and a change from the usual kind of cereal food will sometimes be appreciated. Plenty of milk should be given, but slops are best avoided. The amount of exercise should not be reduced for the first month or so, but after that it should be more sedate, as violent romping with other dogs sometimes proves disastrous to a bitch in whelp in the later stages. Often it is not possible to tell with certainty whether a mating has been successful until five or six weeks afterwards, and so it is not worth while to make definite preparations for the actual whelping until it is certain that they will be necessary. The normal gestation period is sixty-three days, but a day or two more or less is not uncommon, and occasionally there is an even greater deviation from the normal. However, plans for whelping can always be made in good time. The whelping table given at the end of this chapter will be found useful in making one's calculations. Where the bitch is accustomed to an outdoor kennel this is probably the best place for her to whelp, but if she has been accustomed to living indoors careful consideration should be given to choosing the most suitable location for the whelping-box. Specially constructed boxes for this purpose are rather expensive ; a nice, smooth, roomy packing-case from the grocer's will prove equally serviceable. The lid can be dispensed with and the box turned on its side, and a slat of wood two or three inches wide nailed to the bottom of the opening to keep the bedding—and later the puppies —in their proper place. Pine shavings or wood wool are better than straw for bedding, because the sharp ends of straw are apt to damage the puppies' eyes and be irritating to their tender skins. The whelping-box should be placed in some secluded and draught-free corner out of the way of domestic traffic and the bitch introduced to her new quarters. If she appears to be quite happy all is well, but if she shows dissatisfaction it is advisable to investigate the cause, as if she takes a dislike to her quarters she may at the last moment decide to have her puppies in some highly inconvenient spot elsewhere—possibly down a rabbit-hole.

With the near approach of the event there are other details to be attended to. The novice who has had no experience of a whelping would be wise to arrange for the presence of some one who has. But that is not always possible, and if not, it is worth while to acquaint the local veterinary surgeon of the anticipated date of the whelping in order that he may not be caught unawares should his services be requisitioned. Symptoms incidental to a whelping may sometimes cause a novice needless alarm, and on the other hand, dangers which would be apparent to the practised eye would be ignored by inexperienced people. Normally the bitch consumes the foetal envelope covering each puppy and needs no assistance, and the less interference the better. An old, clean sack neatly folded, or a piece of old, clean carpet should be placed on the floor of the whelping-box and replaced as soon as possible after the puppies are born.

On no account should instruments be used at a whelping by any but professional veterinarians, and the newly born puppies should be handled as little as possible. Usually the litters borne by West Highland White Terriers are moderate in number, four or five being usual, so that the question of a foster-mother seldom arises. But if for any reason it is necessary to consider the provision of a foster, there are firms which specialize in the provision of these. The writer is not in favour of their use merely to bring up surplus puppies, but only in the event of the mother herself being unable to rear her family.

Recently the author has seen an artificial foster-mother, with teats for nine puppies, in use at the National Canine Defence League's Animal Hospital at Preston Park, Brighton. This cabinet is intended to replace the living foster-mother in cases where the mother dies or has more puppies than she can rear.

WHELPING TABLE

Date of Service	Puppies Due	Date of Service	Puppies Due
January	March	July	September
1	5	2	3
8	12	9	10
15	19	16	17
22	26	23	24
	April		October
29	2	30	1
February		August	
5	9	6	8
12	16	13	15
19	23	20	22
26	30	27	29
March	May	September	November
5	7	3	5
12	14	10	12
19	21	17	19
26	28	24	26
April	June	October	December
2	4	1	3
9	11	8	10
16	18	15	17
23	25	22	24
	July	29	31
30	2	November	January
May		5	7
7	9	12	14
14	16	19	21
21	23	26	28
28	30	December	February
June	August.	3	4
4	6	10	11
11	13	17	18
18	20	24	25
25	27		March
		31	4

3

CHAPTER V

THE REARING OF PUPPIES

FOR the first few days of their lives the puppies should be handled as little as possible, the mother's brief absences from her family being taken advantage of for any necessary interference. The puppies should be weighed shortly after birth, and a note of the respective weights made on a progress chart. Thereafter, the puppies should be weighed every week. This is most useful in helping to identify the bad-doers, as a healthy puppy invariably gains steadily in weight except that they may stand still for a week or so at weaning-time. West Highland puppies are generally accounted easy to rear, although some strains are rather more delicate than others.

For the first three weeks their entire nourishment will be derived from the natural source. At the end of that period weaning should begin. At first they should be given a small quantity of sweetened cow's or goat's milk. Some breeders who have the necessary accommodation keep a goat especially for the benefit of their dogs. The proprietary milk foods are very good, too—especially if there are any misgivings about the local milk supply. At first the flavour of milk from unaccustomed sources may not meet with the puppies' approval, but by dipping their noses in the saucer their taste for it will soon be cultivated and esteemed equally with the natural supply. This relieves the strain on the dam and within a couple of weeks she will be able to leave her family for hours at a time. At this stage they can be given a daily ration of finely minced raw meat. A teaspoonful for each is sufficient at first, and this can gradually be increased. When seven weeks old their weaning should have been completed, and their diet should consist of four or five small meals a day. Meat, puppy biscuit slightly moistened with gravy or milk, milk puddings and an occasional raw egg well beaten up should constitute two or three of the meals and the other two meals should consist only of milk to drink. The quantities given should be increased very gradually until they are five months old, when the number of meals should be reduced by one. The quantities, however, should be increased to compensate for this. Incidentally, when disposing of puppies of tender age the breeder should make sure that the new owner understands how to feed it. Quite a number of puppies suffer through being wrongly fed or under-fed by people whose knowledge of the matter is sadly lacking. The giving of a fair proportion of hard and dry solid food hastens the process of replacement of the milk teeth by the permanent ones. Large, flat bones can also be given to the puppies to gnaw. Cod-liver oil, being rich in vitamin D, is helpful in overcoming any tendency to rickets. Worm medicines are not necessary unless a puppy actually shows evidence of the existence of these pests—and some of the cures for them are worse than the disease. If worms are seen give one-half to a teaspoonful of medicinal paraffin and avoid quack remedies. Worm-medicine other than paraffin should be given only on veterinary advice, as prescription and dosage are a matter for the expert.

Skin trouble, when it appears, can usually

be put an end to by the total cessation of the
meat ration for a few days, and the giving of a
mild aperient (medicinal paraffin or olive oil,
but *not* castor oil). Where there is irritation
a soothing lotion should be applied to the skin.

When puppies appear to be in need of a
digestive tonic, one-grain doses of saccharated
carbonate of iron are useful.

When puppies are three months old it is
time for them to be house-trained, for this
process does not become easier as they get
older, and well-mannered puppies command a
readier market. West Highlands are one of
the easiest breeds to house-train. The puppies
should be given every opportunity to be clean
by being regularly placed outside first thing
in the morning and last thing at night—and at
frequent intervals during the day. A little
patience and an occasional mild scolding
immediately after, and in the presence of,
any misdeed will soon instil the elements of
good manners into most puppies. In any
event, severe corporal punishment should be
avoided as it breaks a puppy's spirit.

Another phase of training which can be
taught concurrently with house-training is in

coming to heel and keeping to heel when bidden. This is a very necessary accomplishment in these days, when a dog's life often depends upon his implicit obedience to his owner's commands. It enables the owner to dispense with a lead except in crowded thoroughfares and gives the dog considerably more freedom than he would be allowed if he were undisciplined. The first step is to accustom the puppy to wearing a collar or harness —the writer prefers the latter. This can be done, of course, indoors if the puppy objects, as some do, and lies down with his legs sticking in the air. His prejudices against collar or harness having been overcome, take him out in the garden or on some quiet footpath and attach a lead to the collar. The puppy will then probably either gallop ahead or lag behind. The lead should be given a gentle tug forward or backwards as necessary, and the puppy made to understand that he is expected to come to heel and keep there. This may call for the exercise of considerable patience and persistence for a week or two, but a puppy who will keep to heel saves his owner a good deal of worry and increases his own expectation of life by a good deal.

Other accomplishments can come later. A dog's first introduction to water often needs to be performed with tact. It is no use flinging a hesitating puppy into the middle of a pond and expecting him to like it, for he may thus develop an antipathy to water that may take a long time to overcome. Far better to coax him down a gently shelving bank and throw a stick or a ball a little way and then gradually increase the distance. A warm day should be chosen for these swimming-lessons and the puppy should, after being allowed to shake himself, be given a rub down with a rough towel.

A puppy's education is incomplete unless he has been taught to refrain from jumping up at people and from occupying settees, chairs and bed-coverlets except by special permission. He can also be made to understand that flower-beds and borders are made to look at, and not for the performance of canine high jinks or for the interment of unwanted effects.

The problem of selling West Highland puppies does not present such difficulties to the breeder as do many other breeds. For one thing, litters are not over-large, and for another, there has not been any great increase in the number of breeders in recent years. The number of Kennel Club registrations of the breed remained fairly constant for the decade before 1939, and this, if continued, is a happy augury for the future. West Highland breeders are, in fact, in a far happier position than many interested in other breeds. The demand remains steady and, if anything, in advance of the supply. This enables good prices to be maintained and, moreover, one is unlikely to be left with a number of increasingly expensive mouths to be fed long after they are ready to leave the kennels. This only too often happens with over-prolific breeds that quite commonly run to double figures in a litter.

There is one very sound piece of advice that should be borne in mind by breeders, and that is to be wary in any transactions with strangers. There are some shady folk on both sides of the dog-dealing business, and the prospective seller should decline to be persuaded into parting with dogs to any plausible and well-dressed individual who flourishes a cheque-book. This latter may be his own or it may not, but hard cash is much more convincing than any opulence of manner. A similar degree of caution is necessary in dealing with unknown people living at a distance. They may have a high-sounding address and expensive-looking note-paper, but unless their standing can be easily verified it is wise for the breeder to make use of the 'deposit and approval' system run by the doggy journals. It is not a complicated matter, costs little, and in the long run will save much time and trouble over bad debts. The great majority of potential customers, however, will be honest people who expect a fair deal in return for their money and it is up to the breeder who values, and wishes to enhance, the reputation of his kennel to see that they get it. In advertising one's canine wares, either verbally or by means of newspaper advertisements, it is best to err on the side of moderation. Such statements as that your tiny puppies will make champions savour of cheap-jack methods, and whether the prospective buyer believes them or not they will eventually react to the disadvantage of the person making them. One should confine oneself to the obvious qualities of the puppies and their possibilities judged by the performance of the strains from which they spring. To make a definite forecast as to what is likely to happen to them in a show ring a year or two later is almost equivalent to fortune-telling, which is an entirely different line of business from selling puppies. As for the prices to be asked, these should be gauged according to the varying merits of the different members of the litter as one sees them, and should be on a par with those prevailing elsewhere for puppies of similar quality. This can be ascertained fairly easily by studying the announcements which appear in the doggy papers. The fair-minded breeder will resist the temptation to profiteer at the expense of people who have ' money to burn ', as they are likely to be a bad advertisement for the kennel when they find that they could have got better value for money elsewhere. And above all, if you have asked fair prices for your stock don't haggle. Buyers of West Highlands at the right price are plentiful and there is no need for any departure from dignified methods of selling. And when you have litters for sale it is worth while to keep on hand a small stock of brand-new collars and leads. These can be obtained by ordering from the popular multiple shops, and it will usually be found that the people who really come to buy have brought with them neither collar nor lead. For puppies only two months or so old who are to be taken a long distance, it is better that they be conveyed in a box or basket than carried like a parcel under the new owner's arm.

CHAPTER VI

GROOMING AND SHOW PREPARATION

THE West Highland's coat is not a difficult one to keep in trim. The breed rarely needs bathing and many of the leading breeders only bath their dogs when absolutely necessary. A vigorous daily brushing and the very occasional application of a cleaning block (which is afterwards thoroughly brushed out of the coat) are all that the coat needs to keep it in good condition. At a certain kennels near London, instead of the proprietary cleaning block, whiting quarried and prepared locally is used, and the condition of the dogs is a tribute to the efficacy of this substance. But one must be careful not to overdo the use of whiting or cleaning block. Use it just occasionally— before shows, for instance. Too frequent use will cause dryness of the skin and bring skin troubles in its train.

There seems to be a divergence of opinion

about the method of preparing a West Highland's coat for show. Southern fanciers like
to see a tidier dog than those of the North,
and as a consequence the majority of West
Highlands seen at southern shows are—if one
may say so without giving offence to any one
—smarter-looking than those seen in the
country of the breed's origin. This tidying-
up process is mainly accomplished by plucking
with finger and thumb. This preference for
a smartened-up dog seems to have spread
in the early 1900's, for shortly before the
1914–18 war a judge of the breed made it
a *sine quâ non* for success in the show ring that
the West Highland's coat should be shown in
an absolutely natural condition. He averred
that when judging he would always put down
trimmed specimens. The late Colonel Malcolm, too, did not hold with any sort of plucking of the top coat, which he likened to a sort
of thatch intended to keep the soft undercoat
completely dry, even after submersion in water.
He also lamented the fact that many show
judges favoured extreme harshness as distinct
from mere hardness in coats, and that to
obtain this harshness dubious methods ap-

peared to be resorted to, such as the application of chemical substances. Within recent years, however, the application of substances tending to increase the hardness of the coat have been generally abandoned by exhibitors, because it involves not only possible disqualification but also action by the Kennel Club under the dreaded Rule 17, under which offenders and all their dogs may be suspended from taking part in shows. This revision of the regulations has met with the approval of most exhibitors, but one practice is still not unknown, although frowned upon by most exhibitors and judges, and that is excessive trimming. One occasionally comes across dogs at shows whose outer coat is not more than half an inch long. It is obvious that these travesties of West Highlands find favour with some judges, or otherwise their exhibitors would not persist in this practice. It finds no sanction in the official standard of the breed, which lays it down that the coat shall be about two inches long. One wonders, too, what Colonel Malcolm ˙ would have thought and said about a half-inch ' thatch '. It is a pity that there should be such differences of opinion on the matter of coat, which are not in the best interests of the breed. At the present time the smartening-up which the southern show dog undergoes would find no favour in a northern show ring, and conversely the profuse and unruly ' thatch ' that is the pride of the North would arouse no enthusiasm in the South.

The novice exhibitor with high ambitions should be content with a modest beginning, as his first efforts are not likely to be so discouraging, if made at the less important shows, as at the more exalted events like the big Open or Championship shows. Dog showing calls for the exercise of many qualities if one hopes for a fair degree of success, and not the least of those qualities is the ability to take reverses with a smile. If there is no philosophy in your make-up don't aspire to fame as an exhibitor, for nearly all who have made a success of it have had a stormy passage at some period of their career when a stout heart and a sublime faith alone stood between them and the total wreckage of their hopes.

The first step to take is to register one's dog or dogs at the Kennel Club. The next step, which is not absolutely essential but which all exhibitors take if they are wise, is to become a member of one of the specialist clubs for fanciers of the breed. The members of such clubs are imbued with a spirit of mutual helpfulness and the new-comer especially profits from the experience and advice of the older members. Advantage should be taken of the opportunity to attend shows at which the breed is likely to be well represented. There one should get into conversation with as many exhibitors as possible, as a rule they are very willing to give the novice any information that he may desire upon the art and mystery of showing. Watch the various classes being judged in the rings and observe carefully the methods of the different handlers. Try to forecast the ultimate result of the judging— and if your prognostications are incorrect, try to ascertain the reason why. Sometimes the judges will vouchsafe some comment, after the judging, in reply to questions asked by the handlers of unsuccessful dogs, and their remarks are often very illuminating.

The best classes for a novice to choose for his début as an exhibitor are the puppy and novice classes. The Open classes should be left alone until a certain amount of experience has been gained. In the puppy classes the respective maximum and minimum age limits are six and eleven months. Naturally, the older the puppy the better chance he stands, as a very few weeks make a lot of difference.

Having obtained a schedule from the show secretary and made one's entries, it is time to begin the preparation for show. This consists mainly of an intensive course of exercise and grooming—the amount of exercise being gradually increased so that when show day comes the dog shall exhibit that marked degree of strength which all judges look for. There is a point about the housing of West Highlands kept in kennels that has a not unimportant bearing on their show condition, and that is the nature of the runs provided. Grass runs are probably the least desirable in our uncertain climate, and although concrete has its advantages, some of the leading exhibitors prefer gravel runs to any other, as they encourage the dogs to keep their feet up.

As the day of the show approaches it is worth while for the handler to train the dog to stand well and to ignore distractions such

4

as will be found in the show ring—the presence
of other dogs and the close proximity of a
number of people. The dog's teeth should be
thoroughly cleaned just before a show. For
ring purposes a thin collar and a long lead are
desirable ; the latter enables the handler to
stand well away from the dog so that the
judge's view is not obscured in any way.
Handling a dog in the show ring is not an
easy task, and the novice should carefully
study the methods of experienced handlers
beforehand and glean from them all the hints
he can.

Due regard should also be paid to the eti-
quette of showing. Punctuality in arriving at
the show, and above all, in arriving in the
ring at the appointed time for one's classes
should be observed by every one. It is extremely bad form to keep a number of other
people waiting, and unless the judge is lenient
it may result in the disqualification of the dog.

There are some aspects of ring behaviour
in which the novice will be well advised to be
careful in choosing examples to follow. A few
handlers while in the ring contract the regret-
table habit of commenting loudly upon the

judging to their friends and others seated at the ring-side. The great majority of handlers, however, make it a point of honour to refrain from anything that might disturb the judge's concentration upon his arduous and delicate task.

The exhibitor who hopes to achieve a fair measure of success must learn from his failures. Judges are, as a rule, only too pleased to throw some light upon the reasons why a dog falls short of his owner's fond expectations. With such valuable knowledge in his possession the novice is able to guard against making the same mistake twice, and his successes, when they come, will be all the sweeter.

CHAPTER VII

NOTABLE DOGS AND EXHIBITORS

THE West Highland White Terrier's history is mainly one of work and not of show. He only began to be shown in the early 1900's—his first appearance being at Edinburgh—and it was not until 1907 that the Kennel Club accorded the breed a distinct classification. Of the dogs of the early show era the great Ch. Morven was outstanding, both on the bench and as a sire. Another notable dog, a contemporary of Morven, was Ch. Kiltie. Although his success as a show dog equalled Ch. Morven's, as a stud-dog he failed to leave a lasting influence upon the breed. Mr. Holland Buckley's Ch. Nevis was a dog of first-rate type, and others in the forefront of the breed before the 1914–18 war were Ch. Glenmohr Model and his sire, Atholl. The latter, although a very fine dog, was debarred from championship honours because his coat was not of the immaculate white demanded of champions. Strangely enough, in addition to Glenmohr Model he sired another champion, Pure Gem, as well as quite a number of other prominent show dogs, among them being the well-known Lothian Marvel. Other dogs of the earlier days were Mrs. Kerr's Ch. Harviestoun Mab, Mrs. Clare's Ch. Cairn Ransa and Miss Buckley's Ch. White Sylvia. Mrs. Pacey's Ch. Wolvey Patrician was one of the most famous of all West Highland Whites.

Writing in 1935 an observer commented :

' Among the dogs of recent years may be mentioned Mrs. Pacey's Ch. Wolvey Pepper and Ch. Wolvey Peacock, Mrs. Innes' Ch. Brean Glunyieman, winner of five challenge certificates and a first-rate sire ; and the same lady's Ch. Brean Taurie, who is also siring first-rate stock. Miss Shaw's Ch. Columbine Cilean, Columbine Cathair and Ch. Columbine Caraid are notable winners. The Hon. Sybil Hood's celebrated Whitebeam Kennels can boast of such consistent winners as Whitebeam Twinkle and Crystal. The latter is getting on in years but is still winning in the best of company. Mrs. Thornton had an outstanding dog in Ch. Leeside Larkspur, who was recently sold to America, and the same lady's Dick Turpin of Dane End, who won over 100 prizes during his show career, is now the friend and constant companion of Mrs. John Duveen. Other leading lights of the Rowberrow Kennels are Puritan Lad, winner of over ninety prizes and two challenge certificates, Rowberrow Roxana, who during one year recently won more first prizes than any other dog bred by the exhibitor ; and Rowberrow Roland, by Dick Turpin of Dane End out of Rowberrow Runnaduck. Roland's picture, specially taken for this book, graces the frontispiece. Two notable dogs, bred by Miss Smith Wood, are Ch. Ray of Rushmoor and Ch. Roderick of Rushmoor. There are so many other splendid dogs that it is not possible to mention all of them within the space of a short chapter, but among those that spring readily to mind are Mrs. Hewson's Ch. Clint Cheek and Ch. Clint Cocktail, Mrs. Allom's Furzefield Prosper, sire of three champions, and Furzefield Periwig, by Ch. Clint Cocktail out of Ch. Placemore Prosperity ; and Miss M. Turnbull's Leal Patrick.'

For the novice exhibitor who aspires ultimately to compete at Open and Championship shows there is an almost unrivalled array of challenge cups and trophies, which are offered by the West Highland White Terrier Club of England for competition at the various English and Scottish shows. Some of these trophies are open only to members of the Club —an additional reason why the keen exhibitor does not begrudge the modest entrance fee and annual subscription.

During the war period 1939–45 and for some time afterwards, the cessation of the larger and more important shows, and other restrictions, altered considerably the value of the awards. Large numbers of smaller shows were held, and it may be, or may not be, considered that the prize-winning records were below the best standards achieved in normal times. These facts should be borne in mind when estimating the value of wartime records.

CHAPTER VIII

KENNELLING PROBLEMS

TO the owner of one or two dogs the question of kennelling does not arise, as the dog almost invariably lives in the house. But when breeding is undertaken and a considerable number of dogs begin to be kept the housing problem needs careful consideration. The first question to be decided is the choice of a site, and this is important. The position chosen should be one where both kennels and runs will be clear from the drips of overhanging trees, and on ground that is not likely to become waterlogged during a rainy spell. It should be so situated that it will afford no cause for complaint from neighbours on account of the noise made by the dogs. West Highlands are not habitually noisy, but any dog worthy the name will give audible warning of the approach of strangers, especially during the night when some people are exceptionally sensitive to noise. Other considerations in choosing the site are its aspect and the shelter afforded by surroundings. The ideal spot is one with an open southerly aspect, sheltered on the North and East by a wall, building, fence or stout evergreen hedge. As to the actual kennels these can be either sectional wooden buildings or permanent structures of brick. In any event the roofs should be of some non-conductive material such as tiles or asbestos, either in corrugated sheet or tile form. The latter can be obtained in colourings to tone with the surroundings. Sectional wooden kennels are obtainable from reputable firms who make a speciality of these things and stock an extraordinarily wide range of designs and sizes. A number of these firms are represented at the important shows and their exhibits will well repay close examination before launching forth on any considerable venture of the kind. It will not be necessary to make any provision for an artificial heating system in the kennels, as the breed is an exceptionally hardy one. The only occasions when artificial heat is likely to be needed is in the event of a whelping taking place during a spell of extremely cold weather, when the newly born puppies may be in need of extra warmth, which can be supplied by the provision of one of the modern portable oil heaters. One of the most convenient types of kennel is that with a number of separate cubicles ranged along one or both sides of a corridor. Ventilation is an important point and the windows should be of the kind that have a top opening which can be adjusted to suit the temperature. A door at each end is an advantage, as the admission of air can then be better controlled. The floor of the kennels should be of concrete, as it is more hygienic than other materials, but wooden shelves raised a few inches from the ground should be provided in the dog's sleeping-quarters. These should be removable to facilitate cleaning, and should have sides a few inches high to protect the dog from draughts and retain the straw bedding in place. As to runs, some of the leading breeders favour gravel as they believe it to be beneficial to the dogs' feet. But let it be clean, graded stuff of a more or less even size and not the crude 'hoggin' containing small, sharp, irritating particles, and much sand that soon degenerates into mud.

The next best thing to gravel is concrete, but this should be laid by an expert and scientifically cambered to obviate the puddles that will otherwise collect after rain. Bricks are not so good for a run as they are absorbent and do not readily dry. The enclosures to the runs are best made of iron perpendicular railings, although chain-link fencing is very good. But see that it is of the type that has been galvanized after manufacture. Inferior sorts are made from wire already galvanized, and the galvanizing cracks at the bends in the course of manufacture, leaving the way open for rust. If part of the runs can be provided with a roof this is all to the good, as the dogs can have a certain amount of exercise even in a drenching downpour.

For breeding on a fairly extensive scale it is difficult to carry on without paid help, and in fact it is almost impossible if one attends shows as well. In normal times there are well-trained people of both sexes available as kennel-men and kennel-maids, and those who have just emerged from the novitiate stage are often glad to accept a congenial post and render whole-hearted service for the sake of experience.

CHAPTER IX

WEST HIGHLAND WHITE TERRIER

(i) STANDARD DESCRIPTION

(By arrangement with the Kennel Club)

GENERAL APPEARANCE.—The general appearance of the West Highland White Terrier is that of a small, game, hardy-looking Terrier, possessed of no small amount of self-esteem; with a varminty appearance: strongly built, deep in chest and back ribs; level back and powerful quarters on muscular legs, and exhibiting in a marked degree a great combination of strength and activity. Movement should be free, straight and easy all round. In the front the legs should be freely extended forward by the shoulder. The hind movement should be free, strong and close. The hocks should be freely flexed and drawn close in under the body, so that when moving off the foot, the body is pushed forward with some force. Stiff, stilted movement behind is very objectionable.

Head and Skull.—The skull should be slightly domed and, when gripped across the forehead, should present a smooth contour. There should only be a very slight tapering from the skull at the level of the ears to the eyes. The distance from the occiput to the eyes should be slightly greater than the length of the foreface. The head should be thickly coated with hair, and carried at a right-angle or less, to the axis of the neck. On no account should the head be carried in the extended position. The fore-face should gradually taper from the eye to the muzzle. There should be a distinct stop formed by heavy, bony ridges, immediately above and slightly overhanging the eye, and a slight in-dentation between the eyes. The foreface should not dish or fall away quickly below the eyes where it should be well made up. The jaws should be strong and level. The nose must be black : should be fairly large, and forming a smooth contour with the rest of the muzzle. The nose must not project forward giving rise to a snipy appearance.

Eyes.—Should be widely set apart, medium

in size, as dark as possible in colour. Slightly sunk in head, sharp and intelligent, which, looking from under the heavy eyebrows, imparts a piercing look. Full or light-coloured eyes are objectionable.

Ears.—Small, erect and carried firmly, terminating in a sharp point. The hair on them should be short, smooth (velvety) and should not be cut. The ears should be free from any fringe at the top. Round pointed, broad, large or thick ears are very objectionable, also ears too heavily coated with hair.

Mouth.—Should be as broad between the canine teeth as is consistent with the sharp varminty expression required. The teeth should be large for the size of the dog, and should articulate in the following manner :—the lower canines should lock in front of the upper canines. There should be six teeth between the canines of the upper and lower incisors. The upper incisors should slightly overlap the lower incisors, the inner side of the upper incisors being in contact with the outer side of the lower incisors. There should be no appreciable space between the incisors when the

mouth is closed, so ensuring a keen bite ; a dead
level mouth is not a fault.

Neck.—Should be sufficiently long to allow
the proper set on of head required, muscular
and gradually thickening towards the base,
allowing the neck to merge into nicely sloping
shoulders, thus giving freedom of movement.

Forequarters.—The shoulders should be sloped
backwards. The shoulder blades should be
broad and lie close to the chest wall. The
joint formed by the shoulder blade and the
upper arm should be placed forward, on
account of the obliquity of the shoulder blades,
bringing the elbows well in, and allowing the
foreleg to move freely, parallel to the axis of
the body, like the pendulum of a clock. Forelegs should be short and muscular, straight and
thickly covered with short hard hair.

Body.—Compact. Back level, loins broad
and strong. The chest should be deep and the
ribs well arched in the upper half, presenting a
flattish side appearance. The back ribs should
be of a considerable depth and the distance
from the last rib of the quarters as short as is
compatible with free movement of the body.

Hindquarters.—Strong, muscular and wide

across the top. Legs should be short, muscular and sinewy. The thighs very muscular and not too wide apart. The hocks bent and well set in under the body so as to be fairly close to each other when standing, walking or trotting. Cow-hocks detract from the general appearance. Straight or weak hocks are undesirable and are a fault.

Feet.—The forefeet are larger than the hind ones, are round, proportionate in size, strong, thickly padded and covered with short hard hair. The hind feet are smaller and thickly padded. The under-surface of the pads of feet and all nails should be preferably black.

Tail.—5 to 6 inches long, covered with hard hair, no feather, as straight as possible, carried jauntily—not gay nor carried over the back. A long tail is objectionable and on no account should tails be docked.

Coat.—Colour pure white, must be double-coated. The outer coat consists of hard hair, about 2 inches long, free from any curl. The under coat, which resembles fur, is short, soft and close. Open coats are objectionable.

Colour.—Pure white.

Weight and Size.—Size about 11 inches at the withers.

SCALE OF POINTS

General Appearance	5
Colour	10
Coat	10
Size	7½
Skull	7½
Eyes	5
Muzzle	5
Ears	5
Neck	7½
Chest	7½
Body	10
Legs and feet	7½
Tail	5
Movement	7½
Total value	100

(ii) GLOSSARY OF TECHNICAL TERMS

Apple-headed.—A dome-shaped skull as distinct from a flat one.

Apron.—The frill or long coat below the neck.

Bloom.—Glossiness of coat.

Brisket.—Front of chest between forelegs.

Button Ear.—An ear that droops and covers the ear cavity.

Challenge Certificates are granted by the Kennel Club for award at championship shows only, to the best of each sex in certain breeds.

5

Championship.—To qualify for the description of champion a dog must win three challenge certificates at different shows under different judges.

Cobby.—Short in the back like a cob.

Couplings.—That part of the body between the shoulders and hips.

Dew-claws.—The extra claws and rudimentary toes ; they are usually removed in puppyhood.

Down-faced.—A downward curvature of the nose.

Dudley-nosed —Pink-nosed.

Felted.—A closely matted coat.

Hare-foot.—A long narrow foot.

Hocks.—The joints above the pasterns of the hindlegs.

Huckle-bones.—The hip-bones.

In-breeding.—The mating of dogs closely related.

Leather.—The skin of the external ear.

Lumber.—Carrying an excess of flesh.

Out at Elbows.—Having the joints turning away from the body.

Overshot.—Having the upper jaw projecting over the lower.

Pad.—The cushioned part of a dog's foot.

Pastern.—That part of the leg below the knee.

Pig-jawed.—Having a very much overshot jaw.

Roach-backed.—Having a back arched along the spine and especially in the region of the loins.

Septum.—The division between the nostrils.

Snipy-jawed.—Too long and narrow in the muzzle.

Stifle.—The joint next the buttock, corresponding with a human knee-joint.

Stop.—The depression between the eyes.

Timber.—The leg-bones.

Transfer.—The procedure to be followed by the new owner of a registered dog before it can be exhibited at a recognized show. Transfers must be registered at the Kennel Club and a small fee is charged.

Undershot.—The lower incisors projecting beyond the upper.

Weedy.—Too lightly formed, especially in the region of the ribs.

Wheaten.—A pale, yellow-coloured coat.

(iii) Specialist Clubs

West Highland White Terrier Club of England.

North of England Cairn, West Highland White, and Scottish Terrier Club.

Northern District Cairn, Scottish and West Highland White Terrier Club.

West Highland White Terrier Club (Scotland).

West Highland White Terrier Club of America.

Note.—The names and addresses of the respective Secretaries can be obtained from the Secretary of the Kennel Club, 84, Piccadilly, London, W.1.

CHAPTER X

SOME ASPECTS OF DOG-LAW

THE properly trained West Highland is as well behaved as any dog, but there are occasions when even a dog of good character is tempted to transgress, or his owner unwittingly infringes the law. A few remarks therefore upon the various aspects of dog-law may help to avoid conflict with authority. To take what is probably the first question that comes to one's mind—licences. The dog-tax of 7s. 6d. for each dog falls due on the 1st January of each year and applies to all dogs, not under the age of six months, with a few exceptions such as working cattle- and sheep-dogs and blind people's guide-dogs and certain special exemptions in regard to young hounds belonging to a pack. It may sound rather absurd, but a person acquiring a dog over six months old in, say, November is required to take out a licence forthwith, and again on the 1st of

January following. Another point that sometimes leads to confusion is that the owner is
licensed to keep a dog, and that the licence is
not transferable to a new owner.

A dog-law that is infringed oftener than any
other is the Control of Dogs Order, which
requires that every dog while on the public
highway shall wear a collar with the owner's
name and address either on the collar or on a
plate or badge attached to it. The non-
observance of this order renders the owner
liable to a fine and is one of the chief reasons
why homes for lost dogs are so full.

Another aspect of the law that every dog-
owner should know something about is the
rights of dogs on the highway. A dog has as
much right to the use of the road as a human
being so long as he is behaving in a rational
way and using the road not as a playground
but for the purpose of passing and re-passing
upon his lawful occasions. An uncontrolled
dog upon the road who is responsible for
causing an accident to any other road-user
renders his owner liable to an action at law
by the aggrieved party. On the other hand,
the Road Traffic Act requires that a motorist

who runs over a dog must stop and give his name and address if required to do so, or otherwise report the accident to the police within twenty-four hours.

The law regarding trespassing dogs is of considerable importance, especially to owners whose dogs have the hunting instinct highly developed. The onus of excluding a dog from private property does not rest with the owner of the property but with the owner of the dog. The trespassing dog, however, cannot be shot out of hand, and the notices one sees displayed on some private estates that ' trespassing dogs will be shot ' would be more useful as firewood. The shooting of trespassing dogs finds no sanction in law unless the dog is pursuing game or other animals, and shooting is the only means of saving the life of the pursued creature.

As to the old idea that a dog is entitled to his first bite, this is, of course, a fallacy. The law on the subject is governed by the principle of *scienter*, and a person who is bitten by a dog and sues for damages is not compelled to prove that the dog had previously bitten the plaintiff or some other person. To succeed in his action he has, however, to prove that the dog was known by the owner to be dangerous, and his evidence need only show that the dog had previously *attempted* to bite some person or another animal. When a trespassing dog attacks cattle or poultry it is not necessary for the aggrieved party to prove that the dog had previously exhibited dangerous tendencies.

CHAPTER XI

AILMENTS AND REMEDIES

THE table given below makes no pretence to being an encyclopaedia of veterinary practice. It is merely intended to guide the dog-owner in applying simple remedies to simple ailments of the West Highland White Terrier, and in administering first aid in more serious troubles. Some of the references to certain ailments do not mention any palliatives or remedies, because it is imperative in such cases to secure skilled veterinary aid as soon as possible. Indeed, in most of the doggy troubles here set forth it is advisable to consult a veterinary surgeon in the event of failure to secure a speedy response to home treatment.

ABSCESSES. These are painful swellings containing pus usually due to local infection caused by the intrusion of a foreign body. Apply fomentations (not too hot—try them first on the back of your hand) in order to bring to a head, when the abscess should be opened with a very sharp knife which has been sterilized, and then squeezed. Cleanse with a mild antiseptic, say diluted hyd. peroxide, and apply a dressing of medicated gauze and plaster. If a further incision is necessary the same procedure should be followed.

BRONCHITIS. This complaint mostly begins with a cold.

Symptoms.—Cough and difficulty in breathing. The eyes are red and inflamed, the nose dry and hot, mouth dry, tongue parched and coated with brown fur.

On placing the ear to the side of the chest, the rattle of the phlegm in the lungs is sometimes distinctly heard in the effort of breathing.

Treatment.—Place the dog in a moderately warm, ventilated and dry room. Envelop the dog's chest in cotton-wool or apply a coat ; restrict exercise ; administer a good cough mixture ; see that the bowels are relaxed ; and waste no time in summoning skilled advice if improvement is not early apparent. As an outward application, hot linseed-meal poultices or embrocation may be applied to the chest-walls.

Relief will often be obtained by the use of an ordinary bronchitis kettle containing eucalyptus.

BURNS (see Wounds).

CATARRH (commonly known as cold).

Symptoms.—Eyes watery, nose hot, shivering, sneezing, sometimes cough, languor, feverishness and thirst.

Treatment.—Keep the patient warm and comfortable ; the most suitable diet is warm broth, beef tea, or milk.

CANKER OF THE EAR. True canker of the ear is associated with a discharge from that organ, and is an inflammation of the internal or external auditory canals.

Symptoms.—The dog holds the head on one side, shakes it, and scratches the ear, the interior of which is inflamed, with often a brown discharge present.

Treatment. Dry Form.—Put a little zinc ointment into the ear once daily and massage the back of the ear gently to work it in. Clean out every fourth day with a wad of dry cotton-wool on the end of a thin stick.

Wet Form.—Wipe away discharge and clean out ear with a wad of cotton-wool on the end of a stick dipped in lead-lotion to which a little methylated spirit has been added.

In either case consult a veterinary surgeon at an early stage.

Internal canker, if neglected, will cause serious trouble and intense pain to the dog.

COLIC. *Symptoms.*—Great pain in abdomen, and distress ; dog springs up howling, arches his back and is very restless, breathing quickly.

Cause may be bones bolted whole, too much swimming, or severe constipation.

Treatment.—In severe cases, give 6 to 12 minims chlorodyne in water. Consult a veterinary surgeon if immediate cure is not obtained.

CONSTIPATION.   The motions of a dog should be formed and firm, but when constipated it is generally the result of unsuitable food and want of sufficient exercise ; as a remedy, raw meat and liver are laxative in effect, to which may be added a little cooked green vegetable. The addition of medicinal paraffin or olive oil to a dog's food once daily will usually overcome any costiveness, and it is quite harmless and tasteless.   Or a pinch of Epsom salts in the first lot of drinking water each day during warm weather will be found equally effective.

COUGH OR HUSK.   If a dog has a cough (especially a young dog) be suspicious of distemper.   Give cough mixture and proceed as advised under 'Bronchitis'.   If other symptoms follow, the case will probably be distemper, which see.

DIARRHOEA.   The treatment of this complaint in its early stages needs only a mild dose of castor oil to remove the irritating cause.   From a teaspoonful to a tablespoonful of the oil to be given from a spoon, which is previously warmed in hot water, or warm milk could be added to the oil.   The diet should consist of anything that has thickening properties, such as mutton broth, thickened with isinglass, or rice and barley water, slightly chilled.   Egg beaten in milk and thickened with arrowroot or cornflour is very beneficial and soothing.   The external parts should be cleansed, and the bedding kept dry.

DISTEMPER AND HARD-PAD (see also HARD-PAD).   Healthy conditions reduce the risk of both diseases, which are believed to be interrelated. Early symptoms of both are often similar.

Symptoms.—Heavy, sleepy look about the face, nose hot and dry, disinclination for food, shivering, arched back, and general lassitude. In two or three days a watery discharge takes place from the eyes and nose, frequent sneezing, followed by coughing, retching and vomiting. The discharge from the eyes and nose becomes thick and sticky, and the eyelids are inflamed and swollen, the breathing quickened, inclination for warmth more evident, and prostration. All these symptoms may not appear together, and some may not appear at all. In fact, the disease is most variable in its character.

Treatment.—On noticing the first symptoms, place the dog in a dry, well-aired room. If in a kennel, let it be well drained and disinfected. The food should be light and nutritious, such as mutton broth or beef tea, with the fat removed, and milk. If the dog refuses any food, meat, nearly raw, minced and given in the form of small balls, will afford the best support. The symptoms must be treated as they arise, and if one would be successful, a veterinary surgeon should be consulted at once.

Isolate the patient.

A warm flannel jacket is beneficial.

When recovery commences, cod-liver oil and iron greatly assist the process ; the ordinary diet to be resumed with the dog's convalescence. The dog should be regarded as an invalid for at least a week after the febrile symptoms have subsided, as otherwise there is a grave danger of a relapse with almost inevitably a fatal termination.

It is important to note that the discharge from the eyes and nose must be carefully and frequently removed and a little vaseline smeared on the edges of the eyelids.

It is impossible here to say as much about distemper as one would like. There are a number of books dealing exclusively with this scourge of the canine race, which make interesting and profitable reading.

Eye Disease. Many dogs suffer from weak eyes, which constantly water, and often become covered with a white film. Bathe daily with a warm boracic lotion.

White spots upon the glass of the eye often

follow distemper, and sometimes occur early in that disease. They slowly disappear after the illness has subsided, and usually leave little or no trace. The following lotion is very useful for hurrying the disappearance of such spots : Zinc sulph., 3 gr. ; Boracic acid, 10 gr. ; Water, 1 oz. Apply a few drops to the eye daily or twice daily.

Conjunctivitis, or inflammation of the mucous membrane of the eye, is a painful condition in which tears flow copiously and the eye has a swollen and red appearance. The dog aggravates it by constantly scratching it and rubbing it along the floor. Frequent bathing with boracic lotion is necessary, and the eye should be shaded from strong light or the dog kept in a darkened room. The edges of the eyelids may be anointed every night with yellow oxide of mercury ointment.

ECZEMA. This disease, which is commonly known as ' blotch ' or ' red mange ', is a frequent and troublesome affection with dogs. The dog scratches and bites himself in the same way in both diseases, but the principal parts affected in eczema are along the back, especially just in front of the tail, and the head and face, particularly the edges of the lips and eyes. Other parts often affected are between the thighs and under the arms, and on the abdomen, the skin having a very red appearance and which is the form wrongly called ' red mange '.

The principal causes of eczema are want of sufficient exercise, and injudicious feeding. Worms or digestive disturbances are also sometimes contributory causes.

Treatment.—Give opening medicine at the onset—about 30 gr. of Epsom salts or Glauber salts in a little sweetened milk.

There are various preparations for outward use to allay the irritation, but veterinary intervention is recommended in all cases of suspected eczema as diagnosis is not always an easy matter for the amateur.

FITS. Dogs of all breeds and all ages are subject to epileptic fits, which have often been mistaken for rabies—now happily to all intents and purposes non-existent in this country.

Symptoms.—In a moment, when apparently in perfect health, the dog is seized with a fit.

6

Suddenly reeling and falling on his side, violent convulsive spasms attack the voluntary muscles, especially the limbs, which keep up a kicking motion. Frequently a sharp cry is uttered, followed by whimpering. During the attack the urine and motions are often voided, the tongue being sometimes severely bitten, gums presenting a livid hue, mouth filled with frothy saliva, and the eyes prominent. The seizure may only last five minutes, which may be succeeded by the dog lying motionless and utterly unconscious, as if it were in a sound sleep. This state may continue for half an hour or more.

Treatment.—The dog should be secured at once to prevent him running away. The collar should not be tighter than is absolutely necessary, or it may exert pressure on the blood-vessels of the neck. Cold water is the best remedy, and if a tap is handy, turn it on the animal's head. One fit being often the forerunner of others, a veterinary surgeon should be consulted, with a view of ascertaining the cause and the necessary remedy to be applied. A piece of wood between the teeth will save the tongue from being bitten.

Foot Troubles. Of these the most common, apart from accidental injuries, are the troublesome interdigital cysts. The causes are obscure, and in most dogs afflicted by them they reappear at irregular intervals. If left alone they become very painful and render the dog lame until they burst. It is best to hasten the ripening process by fomentations or poultices, and to lance at the appropriate moment. The cysts should be thoroughly emptied by squeezing, and then cleaned with a mild antiseptic. A bandage should afterwards be applied to the foot.

One treatment is to dissolve some Reudel's bath salts in warm water, place in jam-jar and steep the affected foot for 10 minutes twice daily.

Inflammation of the interdigital skin is often caused by the adhesion of tar from newly tarred roads. Where tarring is in progress it is best to inspect the dog's feet every day. Any adhering tar can be easily removed with a little fresh butter. If irritation has been set up it can be allayed by placing the dog's feet night and morning in a solution of one part of methylated spirit to four of water.

FRACTURES. Broken bones are obviously a veterinary surgeon's concern. If sustained out of doors great care should be taken in moving the dog. He should not be carried in one's arms, but on something fairly rigid that will obviate movement of the fractured parts.

GASTRITIS OR CATARRH OF THE STOMACH is often caused by impure or unsuitable food or by an internal chill. The most noticeable symptoms are excessive thirst with vomiting and diarrhoea. The animal is feverish and usually lies stretched out on the coldest place he can find, panting and whining. It is best to disturb him as little as possible. Give barley-water or milk and soda-water mixed, withholding food for the first twenty-four hours. Gastric sedatives, such as carbonate of bismuth, may be given to alleviate vomiting. If the attack appears to be severe, call in a veterinary surgeon.

HARD-PAD (see also DISTEMPER). Inflammation of the brain (epizootic encephalitis). Early symptoms resemble distemper's. Highly infectious ; isolate at once ; take same precautions as for distemper and call ' vet '.

HYSTERIA. A mysterious complaint. Opinions differ as to cause ; most think it due to digestive trouble, others to aural trouble. Many dogs in a large kennel have been known to be attacked one after the other, but this may be due to wrong feeding. The chief symptoms are the uttering of unnatural cries, and an uncontrollable impulse to dash madly around as though in fear of something unseen by others. Often the dog injures himself by striking walls or other objects in his path. He should be at once restrained and given a sedative such as bromide of potassium. It is advisable also to change the diet and to keep the bowels moving with a mild aperient.

MANGE. There are two types of mange— both due to a minute parasite, and both contagious. In sarcoptic mange, the commoner, more contagious and less dangerous variety, intense irritation is set up by the burrowing action of the parasites under the skin, causing violent scratching. Close examination of the skin reveals small red points like flea-bites which eventually become small pustular pimples. These burst and leave the affected parts devoid of hair.

The hair should be closely clipped from around the affected parts. All bedding should be burnt and the dog's sleeping-quarters thoroughly cleansed with boiling water and a good disinfectant. Well wash the sufferer with warm water and soft soap. Treatment is best left to the veterinary surgeon, but it may be said that dressings in which sulphur and oil are the main ingredients form the basis of successful treatment.

The rarer, follicular mange, or scabies, although less contagious, is more difficult to cure. Here the parasite appears to cause more pain than itching and consequently there is less scratching. The trouble usually begins with the appearance of small bare, pustular patches with thickening of the skin. Complete recovery from follicular mange is rare, although many and varied treatments are claimed to have effected cures in individual cases. Diagnosis is very important, and it is very difficult to determine whether mange is sarcoptic or follicular without a microscopical examination.

PARALYSIS. *Symptoms.*—Loss of power and muscular twitchings are the early symptoms.

The affection may come on gradually or suddenly ; if of long duration, wasting of the muscles and emaciation take place.

Treatment.—As treatment in a case of this kind depends very much on the cause of the paralysis, the wisest course will be to consult a veterinary surgeon.

POISONING. The commonest form of malicious poisoning of dogs is by strychnine placed on pieces of meat. The body becomes violently contorted and there is muscular stiffness. Administer an emetic at once—a strong solution of salt and warm water or a piece of ordinary washing soda. As antidotes, olive oil or brandy should be administered and hot-water bottles applied to stomach and back, pending the arrival of a veterinary surgeon.

The commonest form of accidental poisoning—apart from conditions induced by eating unsound food—is carbolic-acid poisoning. This sometimes occurs through using a cleansing agent containing carbolic in the dog's bath, and when purchasing proprietary shampoos it is well to be assured that they contain no trace of this highly dangerous substance.

With carbolic-acid poisoning there is vomiting and diarrhoea, shivering and collapse. While waiting for the arrival of a veterinary surgeon give olive oil or brandy and apply hot-water bottles and keep the dog warmly wrapped up.

Phosphorus poisoning is often contracted through the negligent laying of baits for vermin. It is characterized by vomiting of blood, distension of the abdomen and intense thirst. A solution of 5 gr. of copper sulphate in warm water is the best emetic, and should be followed, as an antidote, by a weak solution of permanganate of potash given at frequent intervals. Oily substances should not be given in cases of phosphorus poisoning.

PNEUMONIA. *Symptoms.*—Shiverings, followed by fever, quickened breathing, occasional short cough, head extended, eyes bloodshot, nose hot and dry, tongue put out and furred, the edges being of a deep red. The animal assumes a sitting posture with forelegs wide apart. On listening at the side of the chest a crackling sound may be heard. As the malady increases, on placing the hand flat on the side, much the same sensation will be felt as though the fluid was boiling underneath.

The appealing look on the animal's face for relief is most affecting.

Treatment.—Place the animal in a warm, dry, well-ventilated room, apply a stimulating liniment to both sides of the chest, and call in a veterinary surgeon as soon as possible.

RHEUMATISM. A common complaint amongst dogs of all ages, which arises through damp and cold, and may be either of an acute or chronic nature. A fixed rule of treatment cannot be laid down for every case of rheumatism, but at the onset it is advisable to clear the bowels, Epsom or Glauber salts being the most suitable, and the affected parts stimulated with repeated hand-rubbings with some mild embrocation. Aspirin is almost a specific, and one or two five-grain tablets may be given two or three times a day. Let the sufferer drink softened water in preference to the ordinary hard tap-water.

Chronic rheumatism is less painful but movements are stiff. In both types keep the dog warm and dry. Massage and radiant heat (with infra-red or sun-ray lamps) are very beneficial. Stiffness will often diminish during walking exercise.

RICKETS.   A very troublesome ailment affecting young dogs, principally puppies, and due
mainly to a deficiency of Vitamin D in the
diet, and to lack of sunshine and exercise.

Symptoms.—Enlarged joints, particularly the
knees, hocks, and stifles, forelegs bowed, and
weak ankles, the hocks turned inwards, making the animal ' cow-hocked '. The bones
of the face often very prominent, giving the
face a swollen appearance. Anaemia often
present.

Treatment.—Mineral tonics, such as iron,
are desirable. Ground-up bones, egg-shells
crushed up very fine, lime-water mixed with
good oatmeal porridge or certain other bone-
forming preparations which your chemist will
recommend are very beneficial, and a teaspoonful of cod-liver-oil emulsion may be given
twice a day with advantage. Plenty of milk
food should be given.

SCALDS (see Wounds).

WARTS.   The dog is rather subject to warts.
The eyelids, ears, mouth and lips are the parts
most attacked, though they may appear on
other parts of the body, especially in old dogs,
and those having white hair.

Never cut warts, as the bleeding causes them to spread. Where there is one single wart it may be removed by tying a piece of silk round the base or neck of the wart. When the mouth and lips are affected, the part should be washed with a solution made of a teaspoonful of washing-soda to half a pint of water, or a solution of salicylic acid. In rare cases the warts call for surgical intervention before they can be got rid of.

WORMS. Broadly speaking, there are two kinds of worms that trouble our dogs—round worms and tape-worms. Infestation with either kind of parasite usually occurs through eating something containing either the worms or their eggs. The sort that usually infest puppies are round worms.

The symptoms are either total loss of appetite or an insatiable desire for food, restlessness, bad breath, vomiting, &c. The passing of worms should be watched for, and no worm medicine should be given unless some are seen in the evacuations or clinging round the anus.

A dose of medicinal paraffin—half to one teaspoonful—every two or three days is desirable as soon as the symptoms appear, and if there is no improvement within a week or ten days, expert advice should be obtained. Above all, do not give any of the proprietary vermifuges unless prescribed. There are a number of effective preparations, but they need most accurate prescription and dosage, according to the size and condition of the dog.

The presence of tape-worm is usually indicated by the passage of segments of the worm. There is accompanying loss of appetite and condition, tight skin and possibly diarrhoea. Worm-segments found to have been passed should be burned. The head of the tape-worm is attached to the dog's intestine, and treatment is directed to making it relax its hold. A vermifuge is given for this purpose after making the dog fast for twenty-four hours. Some vermifuges do not call for fasting. For tape-worms tenaline is highly recommended, but here again the dose should be carefully regulated under expert advice, by the size, age, &c., of the dog. The dose should be followed after half an hour's interval by a teaspoonful of medicinal paraffin.

WOUNDS, BURNS, SCALDS. For wounds, immediate cleansing is the first essential. Apply freely with a sponge or lint a mild solution of some non-irritant disinfectant (avoiding those containing carbolic) until all foreign matter has been removed. The surrounding hair should be cut short with scissors. If the wound is superficial, it may be dressed with dry boracic powder after thoroughly cleansing and will then usually heal without further attention. Deep wounds are difficult to cleanse and if of any extent will need stitching by a veterinary surgeon. When an artery has been severed, the blood flows in spurts and immediate steps must be taken to stop the flow by applying, if possible, a tourniquet above the wound. This is usually practicable when the wound is on a limb, care being taken not to apply the tourniquet so tightly as to cut into the flesh. In other parts of the body the flow from the artery should be stanched by applying a plug of cotton-wool and bandaging or applying firm pressure. In either case the vet. should be sent for at once.

With scalds and burns the hair should be cut away from the affected part, and picric acid applied. This acts like magic in most cases, and is very soothing. Should the burn or scald not make progress within a day or two, the part should be cleansed with a solution of hydrogen peroxide, followed by a further application of picric acid.

Skin Parasites

A search for skin parasites should be regularly made. Fleas run about in the coat, but leave the dog after they have ' dined ' and return to their nests in the bedding, flooring cracks, or skirtings. Sprinkle the dog with a powder containing D.D.T. or 666 ; also the bed and its surroundings. Lice can be discouraged in the same way. Sheepticks need to be removed singly. Smear the skin around the tick with fat to loosen the tick's suckers. If the head remains it may cause inflammation, so wipe away the fat and then dab with methylated spirit.